MW00930723

Cover Design by: https://www.madcatdesigns.net

Edited by: Jessica Peirce

Better Together

A DEER CREEK FALLS NOVEL ~ BOOK THREE

ELLIE RHODES

DOUBLE TAKE PUBLISHING

ACKNOWLEDGMENTS

To Angie and June who are always willing to read through our work in progress and to our husbands who have helped us in numerous ways, as we wrote this book.

CHAPTER ONE

*A*lexis Welby tore open another past due bill and threw it on the mounting pile. With a quick rap on the front door, her best friend Maggie Reynolds-Jacobs walked in. "Thank goodness you're here."

Maggie held up a garment bag. "Don't worry, I have the perfect dress for you."

"I hoped you would, because I spent the last two hours trying on everything in my closet," Alexis complained. "Nothing I have is stylish enough for my date tonight."

As a building contractor, she didn't need an extensive wardrobe. Her idea of dressing up consisted of pulling on a pair of dark jeans and a nice blouse or sweater. She prided herself on her kick-ass shoe collection, though.

She didn't know why she was worrying so much. It wasn't like her to fret over her wardrobe, but then she hadn't gone to an expensive restaurant since she'd started her own construction business, Do-Over Renovations, two years earlier.

"Remind me again why I agreed to go on not one, but *four* blind dates?"

Maggie handed over the dress she'd brought and followed her

friend into her bedroom. She counted on her fingers. "Let's see. One, you haven't been in a relationship for the entire two years since you moved here. Two, you were the one who complained about working too much and never having any fun, and three, you refuse to date any of the men who work for you. You'll never find the man of your dreams unless you date."

Okay, all of those things were true, Alexis thought as she unzipped the garment bag. The dress Maggie had chosen was one of Alexis's favorites, and she hoped she'd look as good as Maggie did when she wore it. She pulled on the form-fitting black knee-length sheath dress and turned her back for Maggie to zip her up. The chiffon bell sleeves added a flirty yet elegant look.

Maggie cleared a space on the bed and sat. "So, who's the lucky guy tonight who will have to remove his jaw from the floor when you walk in?"

Alexis smoothed the dress with her hands. "A friend of a friend of Paige's. I'm meeting him at that new upscale Italian restaurant and wine bar overlooking Lake Superior. He's sending a car."

"He's not picking you up?" Maggie's brow quirked.

"No." Alexis pulled out a pair of black strappy heels from the long wooden rack along the wall of her closet and put them on. "He has a late business meeting."

"Another workaholic. It's a wonder you were able to find a day that worked for the two of you," Maggie said as she handed Alexis a black sequined clutch.

"Ha ha." Maggie wasn't wrong; they'd played phone tag for a week before settling on tonight.

A horn sounded. "That's the car." Alexis slipped her phone, lipstick, and wallet into her evening bag. "Wish me luck."

"Luck! Have fun. I want all the details at the grand opening tomorrow."

Two aspirin and a pair of sunglasses only did so much for Alexis's self-induced headache. She hadn't indulged on red wine in a long time, and she remembered why she'd stopped drinking the stuff. Last night the conversation had flowed, and so had the wine.

The colorful leaves of the sugar maples lifted silently in the breeze, and a large and vocal vee formation of Canada geese headed south for the winter. Normally she loved the sound of the geese flying overhead, but today—way too loud. She released a deep breath, allowing herself to relax. She had done it, she thought with satisfaction. The work she and her crew had accomplished in a short time both exhilarated her and allowed her to make payroll. The Veterans' Center's state-of-the-art physical therapy facility was the first to be built in the northern part of Minnesota. The center sat on the southern part of breathtaking Balsam Lake in Deer Creek Falls, population 948, the small town she fell in love with when just a teenager.

A stream of people entered and exited the Veterans' Center, talking amongst themselves and enjoying the picturesque fall day. Nothing brought the townspeople out like a grand opening. The residents had descended on the building's newest addition with the promise of free food and music. And to satisfy their curiosity.

Maggie ran up to her, squealing. "How was your date?"

Alexis placed her fingers to her temples. "Not so loud."

Cupping her hand over her mouth, Maggie side-hugged her and whispered, "So, good then?"

"Actually yes. Too much red wine, but boy was it good."

"The wine or the man? Did he ask you out again?"

"Both. And no, he said he'd call."

"Well, I hope he does."

"I hope so. I liked him. I'd definitely consider a second date."

A woman with straight, shoulder-length chestnut hair, dark-rimmed eyeglasses, and a brilliant white smile approached them carrying two Styrofoam cups of steaming liquid, cutting their conversation short.

"Hello! I'm Susan Henning and I'm new to town." She gestured to a nearby group of women. "Those nice ladies said you were the contractor and the designer behind this beautiful addition. I thought you two could use a cup of cider. It's quite good." She handed them each a cup of the steaming beverage.

"Thank you. I'm Alexis Welby and this is my friend and designer, Maggie Jacobs."

They glanced over to where Susan pointed to see who the "nice ladies" were. Rosie Cermak, owner of the town diner, and twin sisters Elsie Andrews and Emma Nielson, Maggie's grandmother and great-aunt, gave a little wave. They waved back.

"Yes," Alexis continued. "My crew and I added therapy rooms, the exercise room with swim spa, and the four studio apartments for short-stay residents. Have you toured the facility?" She breathed in the scent of apples and spices, then blew on the cider and sipped. Way too sweet, but she'd drink it because it was nice of Susan to offer the hot beverage on a cool fall morning.

"It's absolutely wonderful. Are the four studio apartments the only housing the Veterans' Center has available?" Susan asked.

Alexis nodded. "Unfortunately, yes. We're hoping for another wing for housing in the future. We don't have many short-term rentals in the area available during the summer months, and the few homes that are for sale would need work to house someone with disabilities."

Susan looked deep in thought. "I see the dilemma. This facility will bring men and women from all over the state, but without housing you may not have a choice but to turn people away."

"Exactly, but between the city and the revitalization committee, we are working hard to provide accommodations to everyone who requires them," Maggie said.

"It amazes me how much a small town like this has done already." Susan gestured to the iron statue near the entrance. "What a magnificent structure. I teared up when I first arrived. It's powerful but evokes a sense of peace and hopefulness for the returning soldiers. I'm from a large military family, an Army brat. Our country's heroes deserve this facility, and this tribute—what an honor to the men and women who have fought so gallantly for our freedom. It's truly breathtaking. Do you know the artist?"

"That would be me, and thank you." Maggie beamed at the compliment.

"You don't sell items at the lovely bookstore in town, do you?"

"I do. That's so sweet of you to make the connection. The bookstore is owned by my future sister-in-law, Paige Turner." Maggie nodded to Alexis. "Alexis remodeled Turner Books and the Eagle's Nest, the local hangout downtown."

"Well, ladies, you are both incredibly talented. I'll have to bring my husband, James, to the Eagle's Nest tonight and check out your work. We just bought the Whitmore Estate on the west end of the lake as an early retirement gift to ourselves, and we're looking for someone with your talents to update our home. We've been dining out or grilling, anything to not spend too much time in the kitchen. But overall, the house is livable for now as we look to hire. My talents lie with teeth. I was a dentist." She chuckled. "When I retired, all I got was a little plaque." She laughed at her pun. "Do you have business cards? I'd like to speak with my husband first, but I can't wait to tell him I met the two of you."

Alexis and Maggie handed their cards to Susan. Alexis swiped her tongue over her teeth, hoping a poppy seed from her morning muffin hadn't taken up residence.

"Thank you," Susan said. "It was lovely meeting you both. I'll be in touch." As she walked away, she waved toward the statue. "Stunning. Just stunning!"

Alexis noticed that Maggie's reaction to the newcomer matched hers. Their smiles grew.

"Can you believe it? This may be the best day ever!" Maggie said.

"I know." *This could be an answer to my prayers*, Alexis thought. "Fingers crossed."

After a long day of small talk and shaking hands, Alexis headed toward the Cup and Cone, or as the locals referred to it, The Hut. The outdoor ice-cream shop the size of a small bedroom resembled a tiki bar and was conveniently located adjacent to the Deer Creek Lodge, close to the local boat ramp. Since Maggie had mentioned they were now serving her favorite flavor, Pumpkin Pie, she couldn't think about anything else. Plus, they'd only serve her fall favorite for a limited time. The Hut closed before the first snowfall and opened for fishing opener in the spring; she had little time to get her tasty treat.

As she drove through town, she noticed a long line at The Hut, so she drove home and parked her truck. Usually, she'd get Zeke to come with her, but he was out of town, and she'd been delegated to take care of his plants. Which reminded her: she needed to water his vast collection of greenery.

Alexis pulled out her phone and texted Zeke. She couldn't wait to tell him she'd met the new owner of the Whitmore Estate.

Hey, it's Alexis. I have news. No worries if you're busy. Just be safe.

He texted back: *What news? Tell me you haven't killed my plants already.*

Alexis pictured the glint in his hazel eyes and the corner of his mouth turning up as he teased her.

She hadn't had time to water his plants in the past few days, and hoped they were still alive. A green thumb she did not have, and she wondered why Zeke trusted her. He knew her tendency to kill anything green.

So sorry. I killed them all.

Now you're scaring me.

BTW . . . I found your last box of Thin Mints. So yummy! She giggled to herself as she waited for his response.

Damn. I thought I hid them better.

Don't worry. I'll replace them with Girl Scout Lemonades.

You know lemon makes me gag.

She laughed out loud, feeling a hundred times better than this morning as she put away her phone and started toward town.

Colorful orange and yellow fall flowers in large pots and window boxes lined Main Street, and all the businesses had some sort of autumn motif displayed in their windows. She stopped to read a flyer on the city bulletin board. Santa Days at Deer Creek Lodge. How could that be only a little over a month away? Alexis waved to several people across the street and said a quick hello to the Sampson brothers, who were out for a ride in their luxury golf cart. They had the nicest cart she'd ever seen: electric purple with a black racing stripe, leather bucket seats, and LED console lights.

Owen Jacobs's black truck pulled up to the curb, and she waited for Maggie and Owen to exit. Owen had married her best friend on Labor Day. Alexis sighed at the thought of having someone who loved her as much as Owen loved Maggie. The two of them worked together as a team on the Lucky Lure Resort, which Maggie had inherited from her grandfather.

Alexis longed for someone to share her love of construction, particularly renovation. And if she was honest with herself, share her bed. Renovating homes and businesses could be dirty and frustrating work, but the sense of accomplishment at bringing old buildings back to life was well worth it.

"Hey, Alexis." Owen stepped onto the sidewalk and wrapped her in a hug.

Maggie hugged her next, even though they'd seen each other an hour before. "I thought we might catch you getting ice cream."

"Ha! You know me well. All you had to do was mention my favorite flavor. I was on my way over there now. Are you headed there too?"

"Maybe later. We're having dinner at Mario's. You should join us."

Alexis's phone rang. She fished it out of her back pocket, held it up, and said, "You guys go ahead. I have to take this. But thanks for asking."

"Text me after your next date!" Maggie called.

Alexis chuckled and answered her phone. "Hi, Brad."

Brad Scott, her foreman for several years, sounded agitated.

"Slow down . . . of course. Keep me posted." Alexis slipped her phone into her pocket. Brad's wife, pregnant with their first child, was in labor. Alexis knew he had planned to take a couple weeks off when the baby was born, but she had hoped they'd be further along on the church remodel.

She approached the window of The Hut. "I'll take a double scoop of Pumpkin Pie in a waffle cone." She'd planned to order a single, but she was an emotional eater. Although happy for Brad, his phone call meant she'd be working more hours, hence the double scoop.

"Coming right up."

No longer hungry after her large dessert, and socially exhausted from the day, Alexis headed for her bedroom to change into her bikini. When she'd remodeled her fifties bungalow, intending to flip it, she'd eliminated the smallest of the three

8

bedrooms to create a large master suite. The day she planned on listing her house, Zeke had bought the house next door. Needless to say, she didn't list. Instead, she added a hot tub and patio, deciding to use her home as a showcase for potential clients.

She grabbed her fluffy white bathrobe and headed outside. She slipped into the warm water of her hot tub, turned the massaging jets on high, closed her eyes, and tried not to think about the longer workdays to come.

CHAPTER TWO

Los Angeles

Ezekiel "Zeke" Reynolds wondered why he'd agreed to leave his sister's wedding reception to babysit, or rather protect, America's sweetheart, who took unnecessary risks. He couldn't keep Mandy Blake holed up in her house any longer. She had an awards ceremony to attend, and a stalker wasn't going to make her miss it even though his threats had escalated in the last couple of weeks since Zeke arrived. Good thing his brother paid well. He had a bad feeling today, and he didn't like it when his spidey senses were on high alert.

Scorching sun and high winds made him wish for fall in Minnesota. As he escorted Miss Blake into an upscale boutique to buy a dress, he scanned the area for any threats. Catching a glimpse in the reflective glass of the boutique's window, he only had a split second before everything went to hell.

Bullets whizzed past his head.

He screamed to the pedestrians on the crowded street, "Get down!"

Zeke tackled America's sweetheart to the concrete sidewalk, landing on top of her. Blood oozed from the searing pain in his arm. "Damn it, not again," he grumbled.

He heard screams and more gunshots. And then the words "Zeke. We got him" came through his com.

"About damn time. Call an ambulance."

ZEKE WAS USED to being away for weeks or months on end, but now all he wanted to do was return home. After getting shot, the only person who flashed through his mind was Alexis Welby. They'd been spending a lot of time together lately, maybe that was why. Who was he kidding? Friend or not, he was attracted to Alexis. What guy wouldn't be, with her sexy-as-hell toned body, her short blond hair, and her kissable lips. But it wasn't just her physical features; she was kind to everyone and always went out of her way to help others.

They'd been friends for a long time, and he didn't want to mess that up. Besides, Maggie would kick his ass if he did. What the heck was he going to do?

The sting from the antiseptic made him wince, bringing him out of his reverie. The ER doctor cleaned his left bicep then gently wrapped his gunshot wound. "I heard you're quite the hero," she said.

Normally, he would answer in a hushed tone, flirting, saying that his heroism was classified. Instead, he said, "No, not a hero, just doing my job."

The doctor smiled and finished with the wrap. "You're lucky it was only a graze." She wrote a prescription for a painkiller and handed it to him. "This should help with the pain. No strenuous activity." She placed a comforting hand on his shoulder.

Zeke's phone vibrated on the tray table. The doctor nodded for him to take the call and turned her attention to dictating notes into the computer.

"Hey, Luke. Everything good?" Zeke said.

"I should be asking you that question. How many phone numbers have you collected from the nurses?"

"Ha ha. None."

"Are you sure you're okay? Running a fever?"

"Nope. I'm fine. Just a graze. Nothing broken."

Luke spoke after a long pause. "I'm sorry this happened."

Zeke winced as he reached for his T-shirt. "Yeah, being shot sucks, but it was worth it. We got another sick bastard off the street."

The doctor glanced at him. A slight smile graced her lips. "A nurse will be right in with instructions."

"Hang on a sec, Luke." Zeke winked at the doctor. "Thanks, Doc."

She nodded and walked out the door.

"Okay, I'm back," Zeke said into his phone. He could hear his brother typing.

"Have you been released?" Luke asked.

"Just now. I need to visit the police station and give my statement. I'll fly out tomorrow."

"I've got it covered. I need you to wrap up a few things for me in the morning, and I'll send my jet to take you to Duluth tomorrow evening and arrange a car to bring you home. You should be back before the evening news."

"Deal. Send me instructions." Zeke's phone pinged.

"Just did. And Zeke—glad you're okay."

The red-haired nurse who had taken his vitals when he arrived entered the room with some paperwork in her hand. "Here are your instructions."

His phone chirped, alerting him of a missed call. Alexis. Instead of calling her, he'd stop by when he got home and surprise her.

CHAPTER THREE

*A*lexis flipped through the mail, adding more bills to the pile, and groaned. The thought of her mounting debt had her wanting to go back to bed and hide under the covers. Instead, she grabbed a zip-up hoodie from her coat rack to ward off the brisk morning temperature. With coffee thermos in hand, she faced the day. She needed to complete a bathroom remodel this morning in Duluth and then check on the progress of the church transformation. The church, soon to be the town's first coffee shop, was the last job on her books for the year. Her only potential lead was the Whitmore Estate.

The income from a job like the Whitmore would help her to become financially stable again. If she didn't get it, she'd need to seriously consider doing something else with her life. Except she didn't know what else to do; she'd only ever wanted to fix up old homes and bring life into them again.

Autumn, her favorite season with its colorful leaves and the smell of woodstoves firing for the first time in months, comforted her. Honeycrisp apples and anything pumpkin were her absolute favorite fall treats. She missed the pumpkin lattes she used to order every fall when she worked in the Twin Cities, but most of all, she missed stopping by a coffee shop before work. As a woman in a mostly male-dominated career, she looked forward to talking with women before heading to the job site. She was beyond excited that Deer Creek Falls would finally have its first coffee shop and that she was part of making it a reality.

With the final payment from the bathroom remodel deposited into her bank account, she drove to the old Lutheran church.

Kate Davis had bought the church on the corner of Main and Church Streets and hired Alexis to remodel it in two phases: first living quarters, then the coffee shop and bistro. Kate, a soon-to-be transplant from Chicago, fell in love with their small town when attending Paige's grand reopening of Turner Books. Kate, an award-winning baker, decided the town could use both baked goods and a coffee shop. Kate's move-in date the week before Thanksgiving gave Alexis a little over a month to complete the first phase. The completion of the rest of the church's transformation was scheduled to coincide with the May fishing opener and the start of tourist season in the spring. Chloe, Alexis's friend, coffee connoisseur, owner of Rural Chic Boutique, and the town's official webmaster, had already started posting "coming soon" advertisements to spread the word.

Alexis arrived at the church to find that the lumber-yard truck had arrived and unloaded materials. Tommy, her student hire, waved to the driver after checking over the order.

"How's it going, Tommy? How come you're not in school?"

"Teacher workshop day." Tommy handed her the invoice. "All accounted for. I have a few more receipts inside for you. They're in the folder you nailed to the wall. I think you'll be happy with the progress."

Alexis smiled at him and took the paperwork. Tommy had proven to be a great addition to her team. "Thanks, Tommy. Let's go inside and have a look." She followed him up the back steps.

Normally she would hear the whining of saws or the pounding

of nails. Today, nothing. Alexis's stomach dropped. *Shit.* "Are you here all by yourself?"

He looked to the floor and then ran a hand through his hair. "Yeah."

"Where's Sean?"

He stuffed his hands in his pockets. "He got a call and rushed off. Something about his mom. He said he'd call you the minute he could."

"Okay, I hope it's not too serious. Thanks for staying. I appreciate you taking care of the lumber order."

It wasn't like Sean to take off without letting her know first. She said a quick prayer for his mom and hoped she was okay.

"So, you're not mad I'm here by myself?"

"Heck no. I'm glad you're here."

Tommy was a good kid, but he'd gotten into trouble over shoplifting small items. Nick, the interim sheriff, had asked her if she would do him a favor and take him on as a work study for a few hours at the end of each school day. The kid was crazy smart and a proficient worker. What Nick didn't realize was that he'd done her a favor by sending Tommy her way.

Alexis walked over to the blueprints and reviewed them. She pointed to the plans. "Let's frame the rest of the walls so Zeke can run electric when he gets back to town."

"Yeah, I wanted to frame, but I'm not the best at reading prints."

"Not a problem. We'll do this together."

Once upon a time, she'd been like Tommy, eager to learn. Tommy took on a task like a duck to water; she only ever had to show him once. Unfortunately for her, Tommy was a senior and would leave for college next year.

Alexis's phone rang. "Excuse me one minute." She stepped away to answer. "Do-Over, this is Alexis."

"Alexis. Susan Henning here. We talked briefly at the Veterans' Center."

"Yes, Susan, how are you?"

Alexis tried to hold back her giddiness. She hoped Susan was calling to discuss the Whitmore remodel.

"I'm well, thank you. Listen. James and I would like to meet with you tonight if you're free. We have a proposition for you. Are you available for dinner?"

"Absolutely." They planned to meet for an early meal. Alexis ended the call and slipped the phone into her back pocket.

Tommy looked up from dry fitting the two-by-fours together on the floor before nailing the wall together. "You're smiling. Good news?"

"I sure hope so."

~

ALEXIS HADN'T HEARD from Zeke since they'd texted after the grand opening. Busy saving the day, no doubt. She had plenty going on as well. She itched to call Maggie and share the exciting news of her upcoming meeting with the Hennings, but Maggie had texted earlier saying she and Owen were taking a quick trip to Las Vegas; Owen had business to attend to, and Maggie was excited to explore the Neon Boneyard and enjoy a couple days with her husband. They'd put their honeymoon on hold until the winter months, when they planned to jet off to some tropical destination.

Although excited about possibly landing the Whitmore Estate, Alexis worried she wouldn't be able to assemble another crew to cover both jobs. She knew she was getting ahead of herself, but she'd always been a planner.

She found a parking space on Main Street and entered the Eagle's

Nest, once a rundown, hole-in-the-wall tavern. Alexis admired her handywork. The previous owner had sold the bar to a man from the Twin Cities, who contacted her a short time after she moved to DCF. The Eagle's Nest was her first remodel in town. With the hip new look, the Eagle's Nest had become a busy and sought-out place specializing in gourmet burgers, live bands, and weekend karaoke. Light rock played over the speakers, people chatted at the bar, and the smell wafting from the kitchen reminded her she hadn't eaten lunch.

Susan waved her over to a secluded table near the back. As Alexis walked past the bar, she greeted her hair stylist and promised she'd make an appointment soon.

Susan stood and wrapped her in a hug like they were old friends. "It's nice to see you again, Alexis. Thanks for joining us on such short notice. This is my husband, James." James stood a foot taller than his wife. He had kind brown eyes, shoulder-length dark hair, and a close-shaved beard.

"Nice to meet you, Alexis. Please, sit." James motioned for her to take the chair opposite Susan. "My wife can't say enough good things about you and your friend Maggie." He motioned to the surrounding space. "I have to say, I love what you've done with this place. I stopped here several years ago for a beer and I remember it being a friendly place, but it was a dive. But this . . . this is spectacular, with the reclaimed wood bar and the black industrial-looking open ceilings."

"Thank you, yes, it *was* a dive," she said with a laugh. Alexis always enjoyed people who appreciated good craftsmanship. She'd take his compliments as a good sign. Before the couple could say more, a young server she hadn't seen before stopped at their table.

"I'm Hannah. I'll be your server tonight." She set down a glass of ice water in front of Alexis. "Can I get you something from the bar?"

Alexis noticed the Hennings each had a glass of beer in front of them. "I'll take what you have on tap from Northern Lights Brewery."

"We have an amber, Lake Lounger."

"Perfect."

"I'll be back to take your order."

When their server returned, Alexis followed the Hennings' lead and ordered a burger and fries. She chose her favorite, a ground chuck burger topped with barbeque sauce, crispy bacon, and melted cheddar cheese, along with the sweet potato fries—a healthier option, even if they did come with a sour cream and maple syrup dipping sauce. The great thing about working construction was that she could eat pretty much anything she wanted and maintain her weight.

As they enjoyed their meal, they talked about the community and how much Susan and James looked forward to belonging somewhere after traveling for work the past decade. Alexis wondered how old they were. They said they'd retired, but they looked nowhere near retirement age. Buying and remodeling the Whitmore Estate meant they obviously had money to spend. Although she enjoyed talking with the couple, she hoped they'd soon steer the conversation to the reason for their meeting. Patience wasn't one of her strong suits.

The server returned, filled their water glasses, and removed their empty plates. Addressing the server, James said, "Thank you so much. That was the best burger I've had in a long time."

Susan nodded in agreement.

"I'm glad you enjoyed it." Hannah left the check next to James.

"So, we should probably talk business," Susan said, and placed her napkin on the table. "We have a proposition for you, something that will give back to the community and benefit the town in the long run." She motioned for her husband to continue.

"As you know, we bought the Whitmore Estate, which has seen better days and needs quite a bit of work."

Susan nodded. "But the estate is livable."

"Definitely," James said, and smiled at his wife. "We decided, after much deliberation, to put our remodel on hold for a while, but we have another idea."

Alexis enjoyed watching Susan and James as their excitement grew, but wished they'd get to the point. She had no idea where they were going with this so-called proposition. She had counted on the money she'd earn from the Whitmore Estate.

Susan continued. "Yes, the estate is on hold because we are at an impasse."

James said, "You do excellent work, Alexis. Please don't take offense, but I'd like to use a contractor from the Twin Cities, someone we've hired to do work before."

Alexis's heart sank. "None taken." She hoped her face didn't show her disappointment and overall sense of death to her career.

"But . . ." Susan said, "after seeing what you've done at Turner Books, here at the Eagle's Nest, and at the Veterans' Center, I want to hire you."

Okay, she might not have lost this deal yet. She sat up straighter. "So, what is this proposition?"

"We've established a non-profit organization and purchased two small homes in town. After they are remodeled, they'll be used for additional housing for veterans who have to rehabilitate for an extended time. We're holding a contest of sorts: James's contractor of choice, and you . . . my choice." She smiled. "That is, if you accept. You'll each be paid to remodel one of the homes. Through my husband's contacts, the houses will be featured in a national online magazine and voted on by the public. We hope the coverage will bring in donations and if nothing else, more businesses and tourists to town. Whoever wins will earn the contract to remodel the Whitmore." Susan grinned. "What do you think?"

"Wow. I'm speechless." Alexis took a sip of her water to suppress her excitement and nervousness. She didn't want to seem too eager. "First, thank you both for the extremely thoughtful gift in support of our veterans. Second, I accept the challenge."

"Great! I hoped you would." Susan beamed with pleasure.

"May I ask about the timeline, and who the other contractor will be?"

James placed his hand on his wife's. "Ryan Anderson of Harmony Construction."

Alexis, having just taken another sip of water, started coughing.

"Are you okay?" Susan asked.

Red-faced, Alexis nodded and coughed into her napkin, managing not to spew water across the table. When she gained control and could finally take another sip of water, she said, "Excuse me." She coughed again. "Went down the wrong pipe." They had to be kidding. Ryan Anderson, her ex-fiancé? What were the odds? She thought she'd left her life with Ryan behind when she was forced to sell her home and move north.

Susan's brow raised. "Do you know Ryan?"

Alexis had to come clean and tell the Hennings. Hopefully, they'd still be okay with the arrangement. "Yes. We dated a long time ago. It's fine, though," she rushed on, "it won't be a problem."

Susan placed a hand on top of hers, which, for some reason, comforted her. "Are you sure, Alexis?"

"Absolutely! Not a problem." She hoped she sounded convincing, but her heart plummeted.

She wasn't sure she'd persuaded Susan by the way the other woman studied her, but James seemed okay with her declaration. "When do we start?"

ALEXIS WISHED she could talk to Maggie, but she didn't want to bother her with her drama, so she sent a text to tell her she had met with the Hennings and that they'd talk in a couple days. She needed chocolate and time to think. On her way home, she stopped at the gas station, filled her tank, and picked up a few boxes of Junior Mints. Popping some into her mouth, she sat back, closed her eyes, and took a deep breath.

She hadn't expected this blast from her past to descend on her small town and wondered how she'd feel when she saw Ryan again. She couldn't afford to pass on the opportunity. If she did, she'd risk losing her business. With her foreman on paternity leave, she'd have to hire another and assemble a new crew. But for now, she'd work both jobs. Alexis looked to the sky and hoped the first snowfall would hold off until well after Halloween. Closer to Thanksgiving would be perfect, but she knew that would be wishful thinking in northern Minnesota.

Susan had given her the address of the house her crew would remodel. She knew the place; she'd passed it many times. The Hennings were scheduled to sign the papers in the morning and would hide the key for her. The family who owned the house had vacated the property. The wife had been the principal at Deer Creek Falls High School, but had accepted a superintendent position elsewhere, and the house had been empty for months. Alexis drove past the house for a quick peek on her way home.

She glanced at her phone. Maggie had texted back with a lot of exclamation points and smiling-face emojis. She chuckled. Maggie always knew how to make her smile.

Satisfied with the property being in favorable condition, she pulled away. A few minutes later, her phone rang, connecting to her Bluetooth. "Hey, Mom."

"I hope you're not too busy."

"I'm on my way home now."

"Are you driving? You know you shouldn't be driving and talking on the phone. I'll hang up."

"No, it's hands-free. I'd planned on calling you tonight. I'm pulling into my driveway now."

Alexis pulled into her garage and switched her phone over. "What's new with you?"

"I'm in town and wanted to see you."

"Really? Why didn't you start with that?"

"I'm at Linnie's. Can you join us for dinner tonight?"

"I've already eaten, but I'll be there. What time?"

"In an hour?"

"Sounds good." She'd fill her in on her upcoming job. Maggie and Zeke, her confidants, were out of town. Her mom . . . the next best thing.

CHAPTER FOUR

*A*s Alexis drove home from her visit with her mom and Linnie, the clouds overtook the night sky and lightning flashed in the distance. She lowered her window to listen to the faint sound of thunder. She loved storms; she always slept better after drifting off to the rumbling of thunder and the pitter-patter of raindrops.

Walking into an empty house normally didn't bother her but for some reason, tonight it did. Maybe she should get a cat. She loved dogs but they needed constant attention, something she couldn't give because of the long hours she dedicated to her career. Maybe she'd add time in her schedule to visit the Humane Society. She could use someone to cuddle with after a long day.

Her blind date from the other night had texted and said he'd taken a job and was transferring out of state. Whether that was true or not, she didn't know. Oh well, it wasn't like anything sizzled between them when they briefly touched. She chuckled at her musings; she had read too many romance novels.

Alexis placed her keys into the metal basket on the island and removed her black leather boots. First a shower and then a bowl of popcorn with a box of Junior Mints to complement the salt.

24

Her taste buds came alive in anticipation of the upcoming snacks. She'd find a chick flick and curl up with a blanket.

She opened the glass shower door, turned on the water, and waited for it to heat. Ice cold. *Damn.* Her water heater had been on the fritz for a while, and apparently the hot shower she craved was no longer a possibility.

She strode back into her bedroom, slipped on a T-shirt and yoga pants, grabbed her comfy pj's and her key ring, and headed out the back door. Zeke wasn't home, and he'd had a multi-jet and rain shower head installed when he remodeled. She needed to water his plants anyway. He had a popcorn kettle and a cabinet full of movies. Why not spend the evening at his place? She grabbed a box of candy on the way out.

The gate they had installed in the fence they shared came in handy. A slight drizzle started as she crossed the yard, but as she stepped onto the back patio of Zeke's house, the rain began coming down in sheets, drenching her while she fiddled with the lock to the back door.

Inside, she kicked off her shoes, stripped off her wet clothes, and hurried into Zeke's master suite. She dropped her pj's on his bed then, shivering, she went into the bathroom and turned the shower dial to hot.

Alexis relaxed under the rain shower, allowing her thoughts of seeing her ex again wash down the drain. Realizing she'd forgotten to grab her shower gel, she reached for Zeke's. Zeke was a good friend, but he'd also been her teenage crush, and lathering her body with his scent made all sorts of past dreams about him replay in her mind. A large boom of thunder rattled the house, shutting down her thoughts. She turned off the water, stepped onto the mat, wrapped herself in a fluffy towel, and headed into the bedroom to find something dry to wear.

❧

Zeke shut the car door, hurried toward his house, and unlocked the front door. He froze when he heard the running water, but then followed the sound and stood in his bedroom, waiting for the bathroom door to open. When Alexis walked out, he cursed and shifted, his jeans tightening. He sure hadn't expected to find her half-naked in his bedroom; he'd only fantasized about such things up until this point. Alexis looked up and shrieked.

"Well, that's a hell of a way to welcome me home," he said, breathless.

Two thoughts hit Alexis. One, she was wrapped in a towel that barely covered her . . . well, all the parts that need covering, standing in front of the man who'd filled her dreams for a long time. And two, the utter desire showing in his eyes as well as his jeans made it difficult to tear her gaze from him. "What are you doing here?" she asked.

"My home. My shower. My towel. Not that I mind, but if you keep staring, I'll have to show you what you do to me," Zeke said with hope in his voice.

"I can see." She let out a soft giggle. Still reeling from surprise and the heat between them, her brain finally kicked in. She couldn't survive the heartache, because Zeke wasn't the kind of man that played for keeps. But hell, he made her body zing with anticipation.

Zeke's phone chimed, releasing her from his spell. She reached for her pajamas on his bed and held them to her chest. If only she were brave enough to release the towel. Would it lure his attention back? But then she'd be playing with fire.

Rubbing the back of his neck, he said, "I need to take this. I'll be in the kitchen."

She slipped her clinging shirt over her head and pulled her

flannel pajama pants on. She'd be going commando for the first time in front of Zeke. But, who cared. He'd just witnessed her in a towel and his reaction—oh boy. She hadn't seen that coming.

She found him in the kitchen. He had just ended his call. "I'm sorry. I should explain," she said. "My water heater went out and since you weren't home . . ."

Her words trailed off as he reached for her. They stood only a breath apart.

Holding her hand, he said, "It's fine. Feel free to use my shower anytime." He winked.

Alexis stepped back. She bit her bottom lip. "Are you up for popcorn and a movie?"

"Sure. I slept on the plane. I'll start the popcorn."

The smell of popcorn had her salivating, or was it the idea of Zeke having his way with her?

"Popcorn is ready."

His voice pulled her out of the visions dancing in her head. Zeke slid a bowl of freshly popped corn across the island.

Alexis remained standing. "Can we talk?"

"I'm sorry I didn't get back to you when you called. I wanted to surprise you." The corner of Zeke's mouth lifted.

"You did surprise me," she said with a laugh.

The tension in the room evaporated when Zeke joined in. "Yeah. You and me both."

He reached into the cupboard for two glasses, grimacing. "Water good? I'm on pain meds, so alcohol is out for me. But I can pour you a glass of wine or if you prefer, beer, unless you finished that off too, along with my cookies?" He smiled.

Alexis walked around the corner of the island. Why hadn't she noticed he was hurt? "What happened? Are you okay?" She placed a hand on his arm and studied his reaction.

"Probably don't want to touch me there. Other places would feel better." He smirked.

27

She slapped him in the arm, and he winced.

"Actually, I meant not to touch me there. I was shot in the upper arm."

"What?" She scrabbled with his shirt, trying to lift it over his head.

"Hold on there, Alexis. If you remove my shirt, I might think you want to go back into my bedroom."

She let her hands fall to her sides. "Can I see it?"

The grimace on Zeke's face turned to a grin.

"Be serious, Zeke. You know I'm a little morbid when it comes to injuries. How bad is it?"

"It's getting worse by the second."

"Omigosh, Zeke. Stand down, buddy."

"You better tell that to—"

"You're incorrigible and looking pale. Can I help you with anything . . . not that." She exaggerated her eye roll and laughed.

"Nope, I'm good. I think I should go to bed, though. Can we talk in the morning? You had something you wanted to tell me but you're right, I'm going to crash, and I want to give you my full attention."

"Of course. Do you mind if I take the popcorn home?"

"Take mine too. Let's put it in a bigger bowl with a lid."

"I'll take care of it." She pointed to the bedroom. "Off to bed. I'll be back in the morning. Text me when you wake."

"Okay. Take the umbrella."

Alexis waited until Zeke headed for bed. She shut off the lights and quietly left, locking the door behind her. Darn. She'd forgotten to water his plants again. Oh well, he was home; he could water them to his liking. The evening was cool and the grass damp as she left with a big bowl of popcorn and thoughts of what could have happened if she'd just let the towel fall to the floor. Trouble didn't begin to describe the thoughts running through her head.

CHAPTER FIVE

*A*fter a restless night of sleep, Zeke sent a text to Alexis: *I'm awake and going to take a quick shower.*

Alexis was swift to reply. She'd probably been up for hours already. *How are you feeling?*

Not as stiff as last night, he answered.

LMAO. I'll bring breakfast.

He chuckled and sent a wink and thumbs-up emoji.

Zeke stepped into the hot, welcome spray of the shower. His joints and muscles were still protesting from hitting the asphalt while trying to dodge a bullet meant for America's sweetheart. He did his best to ignore the spectacular array of blue, yellow, and purple bruises running the length of his left side as he gingerly lathered the soap over his body.

He never dealt in the what-ifs, but this last assignment had jarred him to the core. With his sister, Maggie, married and his brother Ethan on his way to the altar, he questioned the last seven years of his life. After returning home from the service, he hadn't known what to do with himself. He joined the fire department as a volunteer, did electrical work for Alexis and anyone else who needed odd jobs done, and kept himself busy by working security for his brother Luke. Three different professions kept the boredom at bay, but he realized he needed more. His nieces were almost teenagers, Maggie had hinted at starting a family, and he guessed Paige and Ethan would be close behind.

Did men have biological clocks? He never thought he'd settle down and start a family before now, but if he did, he'd like his kids to grow up with their cousins. When he danced with Alexis at Maggie's wedding, holding her close had stirred something deep inside. He had put it out of his mind because he had a job to do, but now, standing under the spray of the shower, he thought of only one woman. The sexy contractor who'd crept into his dreams last night.

He turned the shower knob to cold and rinsed off, then stepped out and slipped into his boxers. With a grin on his face, he replaced the towel around his waist and removed the bandage from his arm. He'd have Alexis help him rewrap the wound and if things got out of hand, maybe she'd wrap something else.

THE SOUND of the shower heightened Alexis's senses. The thought of Zeke and that toned chest of his, naked under the running water, had her mind traveling places it had no business going. They were friends, only friends, she repeated to herself. Zeke flirted with everyone, including Paige back when she started dating his brother. But his reaction earlier gave Alexis pause. Ridiculous. He didn't think of her in that way, or he would have made a move.

Zeke strode into the kitchen, wrapped in a towel. The lines etching his face showed he was hurting. She winced at the site of the colors covering his side and torso.

"Alexis. I need your help."

The pain around his eyes melted her heart. "Anything. What can I do?"

"Follow me."

She followed him into his bedroom.

Zeke pulled the towel from his waist. She gulped and inadvertently licked her lips at the sight of him in his tight black boxer shorts. When he shot her a lascivious smirk, she couldn't help but roll her eyes. Typical Zeke, always trying to elicit a reaction from her.

"I need you to rewrap my arm." He handed her a roll of gauze.

"Huh?" She really needed to focus. "Okay." Their fingers brushed as she took the roll from his palm. She wrapped his injury and taped the gauze in place. "Next time you shower, let me help you."

The shit-eating grin on his face made her realize what she had said. Her face heated. "I mean . . . I'll help you wrap the bandage with plastic wrap before you take a shower. Come on, I made breakfast, and it should still be hot. Put some clothes on."

Both hungry, they consumed their breakfast in comfortable silence.

"Sorry, I should have texted I was on my way home last night." Zeke set his empty coffee cup on the island. "Not that I didn't like the surprise."

Alexis could feel her face flush and cursed her fair skin. "Did you sleep well?"

"Could have been better," he said. "Tell me your news."

Alexis threw the wrappings away and stacked the empty containers to take back home. "I met with the new owners of the Whitmore Estate," she said over her shoulder.

"Did they hire you?"

"Yes and no."

"Either they did or they didn't."

"It's a little more complicated than that." She filled Zeke in on meeting Susan at the Veterans' Center grand opening and the subsequent meeting at the Eagle's Nest.

"Wow, they bought two homes. That's impressive. I don't see the problem, though; who cares if they bring a contractor in from the Twin Cities? You'll win hands down."

Alexis leaned against the sink. "I'm not worried about winning on my ability. I know I can design the better home."

Zeke stood, winced, and walked to his recliner. "So, what's the problem?"

Alexis followed and sat on the edge of the couch, facing him. "The competing contractor is my ex-fiancé, and he's my ex for a reason."

ZEKE KNEW Alexis had been engaged once upon a time, but never heard what happened.

"I started on Ryan's crew, working new construction," Alexis explained. "We got engaged, and then he slept with someone else." She shrugged. "I broke it off, made a few bad business decisions, sold my house, followed Maggie to Deer Creek Falls, and opened a remodeling business. I haven't looked back since."

"Is that why you don't date? Because . . . not all guys cheat."

"I've dated. And yes, I know they're not all two-timers. In fact, I went on a date while you were in California. Your sister and the girls talked me into going on four blind dates. One down, three to go."

A jolt of jealousy surged through him. "I'm sorry you'll have to deal with that asshat of an ex again. Let me know how I can make his life miserable."

"Thanks." She smiled. "I'll let you know." Alexis relaxed back into the comfortable couch. "I've put it all behind me. He did me a favor. Of course, I didn't look at it like that at the time, but if I hadn't discovered his infidelity, I wouldn't have moved here. I love my life, this town . . . I have no regrets. My dad would be proud of me for building a foundation here."

"I believe that too, but I know he was proud of you no matter what. You can see it in that photo you keep on your mantel, the one where the two of you are standing in front of that tree fort you built together."

Alexis's eyes welled up. "We both loved building that tree fort."

Zeke cleared his throat. "So, back to Ryan. Why is he remodeling a house here, of all places?"

"Small world? The Hennings said he's done work for them in the past." Alexis shrugged. "Don't worry, we'll win."

"Thatta girl." He knew she couldn't resist a competition, and he had no doubt she'd win this one. The saying "I am woman, hear me roar" fit Alexis perfectly.

Zeke turned slightly and smirked. "I can't wait to meet the Hennings and your ex. But there's something else on your mind, so out with it."

Alexis tucked one leg under the other and sighed. "I've already started the renovation on the church for Kate Davis, the contest house starts in a few days, and I don't have enough crew to handle both projects. Brad's wife had the baby, so I'll be overseeing both jobsites." She paused to gather her thoughts. "I put a call in to my former foreman from Minneapolis, but I haven't heard back. I don't know how I'll be able to handle everything, but I need to. I need the money." Alexis fiddled with a string on her sweater.

Zeke sat up straighter in his chair. "I'll help. I can run from jobsite to jobsite and assist with anything I can. I'll take care of the electric on both places. Plus, I've picked up a few skills working with you and Maggie. Let me help out."

"Are you sure? What if you're called away again to help Luke?"

Zeke pulled out his phone, his fingers flying over the keyboard. "I told Luke I won't be available until the beginning of the year."

"With what I'm making on these two remodels, I'll be able to pay you well."

"I'm not worried about the money."

He'd known Alexis long enough to know she *was* worried. He hoped she'd let others help. She wasn't alone; she had his entire family and town cheering her on.

CHAPTER SIX

The next morning, Alexis carried two pans of marshmallow crispy treats to the fire station and set her bars on the table with the other snacks, then went to join the revitalization committee near the bay doors. A line of lawn chairs, set up parade style, faced the fire engines instead of the road.

Emma had come up with the brilliant idea to sell calendars to raise money for Santa Days, an annual event hosted by the Reids, who owned the Deer Creek Lodge. Proceeds from Santa Days went toward funding the local shelter and buying gifts for children in need. A local photographer had her equipment set up, waiting to photograph the firefighters.

Alexis joined Maggie and Emma. "When does the show start?"

"Any minute now." Emma rubbed her mitten-clad hands together.

"Do you think it's bad we're ogling them for our own personal pleasure?" Maggie asked.

"Dearest Maggie." Emma placed a hand on her arm. "If you grew up in the sixties, you'd know women have earned the right to ogle men. Besides, it's for charity." Emma grinned. "Remind me to tell you about the Women's Liberation Movement, the day we marched down Wall Street, and what we called the First National Ogle-In."

"Sounds intriguing, I love your stories."

Maggie handed her a program of sorts. "They'll be photographed in order. January through December. Chloe printed these up so we would know who to expect and when."

Glad to have her friend back in town, Alexis skimmed the sheet and noticed Zeke would be photographed for June and Mitch for July. She swallowed the lump in her throat.

Emma nudged her. "I heard you have a date tomorrow with Mitch. Here I thought you only had eyes for Zeke."

"How did you know?"

Elsie wandered over. "Know what, dear?"

Alexis looked over the heads of the matchmaking twins to Maggie for help. "How did you know I had a date with Mitch?"

"Oh, that." Elsie tsked and waved her hand in dismissal.

Paige hurried through the open firehouse bay doors. "Did I miss anything?"

Alexis turned her attention to Paige, hoping Elsie and Emma wouldn't continue their line of questioning. "Nope. They haven't started."

A large crowd had formed, and more chairs were placed on the grass. Hopefully there wouldn't be a fire call.

"I told the men if they walked past us, we'd make sure they earned money up front," Emma said.

With that declaration, some of the women fanned themselves.

Lily Chen and Chloe Reid appeared from behind one of the red engines with smiles on their faces. Alexis hadn't noticed a speaker and microphone until Chloe started the dance music and Lily's voice rang out over the sound system. Alexis covered her mouth to hide her laughter.

"Okay, everyone. First up, we have Mr. January."

The crowd went nuts, waving their arms and moving their hips to the music. Even Mr. January swayed his hips to the beat, having fun.

Wearing full turnout gear, the fifteen-year veteran of the fire department held a Pulaski over his shoulder in front of a green screen. The photographer posed him several ways and then sent him to strut in front of the ladies so they could place money in his overturned helmet.

Paige nudged Alexis. "The runway walk idea . . . so hot."

The fire department wouldn't need to produce a calendar to reach their fundraising goal if the amount of money collected by the first firefighter carried on across the rest of the year's participants.

Alexis had been so busy she'd missed the last couple of organizational meetings. Maggie had asked her to bring twelve five-dollar bills, and she'd figured they were for making change when selling the treats. She now understood.

Susan Henning, their newest resident and her client, pushed forward and threw a fifty-dollar bill into the mix. Everyone high-fived her and Alexis started to relax. She'd never got into the strip club scene and had only been to one for a bachelorette party. It wasn't like she didn't enjoy looking at the men, she just didn't know how to act around a crowd of screaming, hormonal women.

Maggie bumped hips with her and whistled loudly over the crowd. "Nice!"

The men posing for February and March were the oldest members of the crew. They were well toned for their age even though their hair was mostly white, but Maggie was right; they were nice-looking for men old enough to be their fathers.

Mr. April came out carrying a black Labrador puppy. The puppy awarded the shirtless firefighter kisses, and the spectators went wild. Lily announced that April was pet-adoption month, and the little guy was available for adoption.

Mr. May wore a turnout jacket but was shirtless underneath. Alexis had seen the young guy around town but had never met him. If she remembered right, he had graduated high school last year.

Lily introduced June, and Alexis tucked her bottom lip between her teeth. Zeke swaggered out wearing red suspenders over a tight long-sleeved T-shirt that hid his bandage but still showed off his sculpted muscles, carrying a coil of hose around one of his massive shoulders. He tipped his helmet to the crowd and winked at her. She glanced at Elsie and Emma, who clapped and cheered him on with respect. Elsie gave her a thumbs-up. Although she could see her breath in the cool autumn air, she began to overheat. Zeke walked a bit stiffly because of his bruising, but his injuries didn't make his poses for the camera any less mesmerizing. She imagined him tangled up in the bedsheets next to her, his strong thighs on display and her head resting on his tight abs. If she had a hundred-dollar bill, she'd have slipped it into his waistband.

"Mr. July is the newest member of DCF's fire department. Give a round of applause for Mitch Collins," Lily announced. The dance music kicked up a notch and everyone stayed standing. The rumble of an engine made heads turn as Mitch rode up on a motorcycle. Holy hell. His beautifully inked biceps and six-pack were on display. The sight of him in only yellow pants and black boots made Alexis's mouth go dry. Mitch had been Chloe's pick for a blind date. She'd given him Alexis's number, and he had called her last night to set up a date. They'd agreed to have dinner.

After the confusing confrontation in Zeke's bedroom, she wasn't sure where she and Zeke stood in their relationship. Just when she thought Zeke was interested in being more than friends, he had pulled back. Sure, he'd flirted, but that was what Zeke did best. Maybe going out with Mitch was what she needed to get her head back on straight and forget about anything happening between her and Zeke. They were friends. That was it. And there wasn't any harm in having a little fun, especially with a guy who looked like Mitch.

Maggie nudged her. "You had better call me tomorrow and tell me all about your date."

ZEKE STOOD next to the water truck, watching Alexis. Their eyes met and she smiled. He nodded, then disappeared into the firehall, heading for the locker room to change.

Mitch, the new guy, entered the locker room, laughing with the other guys.

"Enjoy your date tomorrow, Mitch," someone yelled.

Mitch sat down beside Zeke. "Thanks, man!" he yelled back.

"Anyone I know, Collins?" Zeke asked.

"Yeah, Alexis Welby. You work with her, right?"

"Yeah. I work with her."

"Any advice?"

"Nope. Catch ya later." Zeke threw his gear in his locker, slammed it shut, and snuck out the back. He had to get back to the jobsite. He'd spend the rest of the day taking his frustrations out by pulling wire at the church.

WHEN ZEKE ARRIVED at the church, he was the only one there. He started to drill holes and place electrical boxes in the newly framed bathroom.

"Hey, Zeke," Tommy greeted him, strapping on a tool belt.

Zeke stepped off the ladder. "You want to help run wire? I can show you and then I can continue on to the rest of the rooms."

"Yeah, for sure."

He had to hand it to Alexis for hiring Tommy; the kid worked hard and caught on quick. Most teenagers had their noses in their phones, but not Tommy. He hadn't seen him reach for his phone yet. After setting Tommy up with running the correct wire, Zeke started on the living room.

After a while, Tommy joined him in the living room. "Bathroom's done," he said. He stopped in his tracks and turned bright red when Sloane Bishop, whose father owned the local hardware store, walked through the door.

Zeke looked back and forth between Sloane and Tommy.

"Hey, Sloane. What do you have for us?" Zeke asked.

Sloane held up a paper bag. "Dad said Alexis needed some supplies and asked if I'd drop them off. Light switches, outlets, and covers." She stopped in front of Tommy. "Hi, Tommy."

Zeke glanced at the teen, who grumbled something incoherent.

Zeke came to his rescue and reached for the bag. "Thanks, Sloane. Are you two in the same classes?"

She tucked her hair behind her ear, and Zeke noticed Tommy swallow. He didn't blame the kid. When Alexis played with her hair, he had the same reaction.

"We have English together." She smiled. "We're both seniors this year."

Zeke bumped Tommy's shoulder. "Cool."

"Well, I better get back to the store. I have a few more deliveries to make."

"Thanks, Sloane," Zeke said.

Sloane smiled, then waved to Tommy as she walked out the door.

"Well, someone has the hots for Sloane." Zeke bumped shoulders with Tommy again and almost knocked him over.

Zeke smirked, remembering the awkward stage of liking a

girl. Of course, by his senior year, he didn't need help finding a date.

Tommy shuffled his feet and slung his bangs out of his face. "She's out of my league. She's dating the captain of the football team."

Zeke felt bad for him. When he was Tommy's age, he had relied on his humor and his wicked flirting skills. But there were girls out of his league, too, and he knew exactly how Tommy felt. Every guy had a Sloane in their life. Teenage hormones sucked.

"You might be surprised." Zeke shrugged. "Be her friend. It may turn into more."

CHAPTER SEVEN

*T*he doorbell rang. "Maggie, he's here. I'll text you after the date. Gotta go." Alexis disconnected from her best friend and shoved her phone into her purse.

She opened the door to find Mitch in a Minnesota Vikings jersey and jeans, his blonde hair tousled like he had just woken up. *This is what he wore on a date?*

"Hi, Mitch. I think I'm overdressed." Alexis had chosen an off-the-shoulder emerald green cashmere sweater, dark jeans, and black heeled boots.

Mitch's eyes skimmed her body from head to toe. "Heck no. You look fantastic."

Alexis blushed. Her first impression might have been too judgmental. He did say to dress casual, and obviously he liked his sports team. She locked her house and followed him to his truck, where he opened the passenger door for her. *One point for being a gentleman.*

She buckled her seat belt and asked, "What's the plan?"

Mitch looked at her with confusion. "Oh. We're headed to Willow Creek to Buster's Bar and Grill. They have a great selection of beer and apps."

When he said Buster's, it dawned on her: Sunday afternoon. He was wearing a football jersey . . . He was taking her to watch the Vikings game. It wasn't like she hated football, but on her one day off and only the second date she'd been on in like, forever, watching the Vikings game wasn't her idea of a fun afternoon.

She faked a smile. "Great."

MITCH OPENED the door to Buster's for her to enter. *Another point for manners. Maybe it'll be fine.* "Thank you," Alexis said.

The noise of the patrons hit her first, followed by the smell of grease. He moved in front of her and pointed to a high table, the only one available. He hurried to the table and glanced at the multiple televisions taking up space on every wall. "I made a reservation, otherwise we'd be stuck at the bar since the game is about to start."

"I didn't know they reserved tables on game day."

"Not for everyone. I know the owner."

The voices grew louder as the Vikings took the field. She couldn't help looking around at the sea of purple. Maybe she shouldn't be wearing green. *Shit.* She was wearing the enemy colors. At least Mitch was kind enough not to say anything. There was only one other couple in the bar who wore rival jerseys.

A twenty-something in a low-cut purple shirt and *short* jean shorts approached their table. "What can I get you two?"

The server gave Alexis a once-over and one of her brows hit her hairline. Alexis already knew she had made a mistake wearing green, but she wondered why she deserved the look she'd received. She raised her voice over the crowd. "What do you have on tap?"

The girl smacked her gum and listed the extensive beer choices. Alexis interrupted her when she mentioned Loon Lager.

"Tall or short?" the server asked.

"Tall, please."

Mitch ordered a beer and picked up the menu. Without even asking her opinion, he ordered four different appetizers.

When the waitress left, he said, "I figured you'd like one of them."

"You made great choices. I like them all."

She wondered if he'd even heard her, because he stood, cursed, and screamed at the multiple televisions, dropping into negative points on her scale.

The waitress brought their beers, sloshing some on the table. Alexis reached for a napkin and wiped up the mess. Their server had moved to the next table before she could ask for a glass of water.

Mitch settled back into his seat. "I can't believe they got to our quarterback."

"Yeah. Somebody on our offense missed the assignment," Alexis said. Her knowledge of football made him smile.

"So, you're a football fan?"

"I like most sports. Football, baseball, women's basket—"

"Oh, come on!" Mitch shot out of his seat again.

He sat back down and in one gulp, finished off half a beer and signaled for the waitress.

Alexis sipped her drink and glanced up at the television. There was a flag on the field. The network cut to a commercial break.

"Sorry, Alexis, I get a little carried away," Mitch said.

"It's fine. How long have you been on the fire department?"

"A few months only. I moved here from Rochester."

She followed Mitch's gaze to the television; the game had resumed with a replay. The opposing team kicked off and the Vikings fumbled the ball. She didn't get a chance to ask Mitch why he'd moved to their town, and really, she didn't care.

Mitch was on his feet again, screaming obscenities. He just missed the waitress with his flailing arm as she set down their food. At least their plates hadn't landed on the floor, but Alexis's shirt wasn't so lucky. She pulled a buffalo wing off her sweater and placed it back on the plate.

Alexis downed her beer while Mitch remained standing. "I'm going to the restroom," she said. "Be right back."

"Sure. Sure."

She grabbed her purse and looked around for the restrooms. Making her way through the crowd wasn't easy, and her shoes were sticking to the floor, but when she made it to the hallway that housed the restrooms and the back exit, she breathed easier. The noise in the hallway wasn't as harsh. She pushed the door open, went to the sink, and rinsed off her sweater the best she could. Even the speaker in the bathroom had the game on. At least it wasn't blaring. She looked in the mirror, fluffed her hair, and applied more lip gloss. Maybe she could slip out the back? But how would she get home? Why hadn't she insisted she meet him somewhere? Clearly, she was off her game and not remembering the rules for first dates. She sighed and opened the door.

"Alexis? What are you doing here?"

ZEKE ALMOST COLLIDED with Alexis as she exited the bathroom. His eyes roamed over her. Her sweater clung to her like a glove, and her boots—all kinds of sexy.

"I'm actually on a date," she said. She shuffled her feet and looked over her shoulder. He couldn't believe Mitch had brought her to a bar to watch the football game on their first date. Seeing Alexis looking toward the exit instead of the bar made him happy. Shutting Mitch down when he had asked him if he had any pointers had been his best decision ever.

Zeke pointed toward the bar. "The bar's that way, or are you trying to escape?"

One corner of her mouth curved up. "Yes. I guess I am."

Interesting. "Not going well?"

Alexis pulled the hem of her sweater out. "You mean besides me wearing a Packers sweater at a bar full of Vikings fans?"

He burst out laughing and couldn't stop, even as she stuck her hands on her hips.

"Are you done?" she asked.

"I take it he didn't tell you where he was taking you?"

"Oh yeah. He did. Halfway here." She pointed at him. "Stop laughing."

"So, if he drove you here, what's your plan of escape?"

"First, I thought I'd get out of the noise and enjoy the sunshine out back."

"Not much to see out back. A smelly dumpster and a bunch of pallets. And second step?"

"To call someone to come and get me."

"Not a bad idea. Except Maggie's shopping with Mom, and the rest of the family are all watching the game."

"Chloe's probably home. Plus, this date was her idea."

"Oh yeah?" He set his electrical bag down and waited.

Alexis crossed her arms over her chest, drawing his eyes lower. "What are you doing here?" she asked.

"The owner called me in a panic. His freezer lost power. Are you serious about getting out of here?"

Alexis sucked in her bottom lip, and he wished she was sucking on his lip instead. "Yes. Can you take me home?"

"I'd love to."

"Let me text Mitch. He probably hasn't noticed I'm gone."

"Impossible."

He couldn't help but read her text: *I'm not feeling well. I ran into someone who can take me home.*

Zeke pulled his keys from his pocket. "Here. Truck's in the back. Give me a minute and I'll be right there."

ALEXIS COULDN'T BELIEVE her luck. Not that she was happy to be laughed at, but now she could get home, do some laundry, and salvage her only day off.

She watched Zeke in his faded jeans and long-sleeve blue Henley exit the back door with a smile on his face. Alexis smiled back. How could she not? His smile and the hint of laugh lines starting at the corners of his eyes were contagious.

Zeke stowed his supplies in the back and lifted himself into the cab of the truck. She didn't know how he took girls on dates, especially if they wore tight skirts, which most of the girls he dated, did.

"Mitch noticed me and waved," he said. "I waved back. Looked like he was checking his phone."

Alexis pulled her phone out and pulled up a text from Mitch.

"Unbelievable." She shook her head and turned the screen toward Zeke. A thumbs-up emoji.

That was it: thumbs-up. Not "I hope you feel better" or "You should have told me, I would have taken you home." Men.

Zeke pulled out of the gravel parking lot and onto the paved highway, traveling in the opposite direction of home.

Alexis looked at him. "Zeke? Where are we going?"

"You're all dressed up, so I'm taking you on a real date."

WHEN ZEKE HAD STEPPED into the bar to talk with the owner, he'd noticed Mitch grabbing the waitress's ass. She responded with a flirtatious smile. Zeke refrained from heading over there to have a discussion on how to treat women. Instead, he waved with a smirk on his face, knowing Alexis was waiting for *him.*

He placed a call to his favorite restaurant. One he hadn't taken any of his dates to before. He wanted to show Alexis how a real man treated a woman on a date. He headed to the next town over, which bordered a small lake. The restaurant was known for their walleye dinners. The weather, a perfect fall day with the colorful leaves and only a slight breeze, would be perfect for sitting on the deck overlooking the lake.

Alexis turned slightly in her seat. "Not that I don't appreciate the irony in this, but seeing as I'm already in the truck with you, I have to ask, where are we headed?"

He chuckled. Alexis always made him laugh. "To my favorite restaurant. The Lakeside Inn."

"Now that is a place I can get excited about. I still have never been. You've talked about it several times."

"I'm sorry I've never taken you there before now. My favorite is the parmesan-crusted walleye with stone-ground mustard, creamy garlic mashed potatoes, and grilled asparagus. But their Scottish salmon stuffed with crab meat, garlic chive mashed potatoes, and steamed broccoli is a close second."

Alexis wiped her mouth. "I think I just drooled."

"Over me or the anticipation of the best fish dinner around?"

"Maybe a little of both."

ALEXIS COULDN'T BELIEVE she'd said that out loud, but the way Zeke looked at her, she knew he was pleased by her response.

When they arrived, the hostess guided them through an outdoor seating area larger than the one inside, set up on an expansive deck that abutted the lake. Lights were strung from post to post, and heat lamps were scattered around. Melodic incidental music played over the speakers. Zeke kept his hand on her lower back as they were escorted to their seats, and he pulled out her chair for her when they arrived at their table.

"This is beautiful." She gestured to the sugar maples, their orange, red, and yellow leaves contrasting majestically against the clear blue sky and reflecting their bright colors in the water. The scattered birch trees lifted their leaves with the breeze. Relaxing in her seat, she followed a red-tailed hawk across the sky with her eyes, his screeching call echoing above.

Alexis glanced at Zeke. He was watching her. "What?"

"You're beautiful."

She was prevented from responding with a quip by the arrival of their server, who brought glasses of water and handed each of them menus.

"Our special today is an almond-crusted walleye with stuffed hash browns and grilled broccoli. The soup is New England clam chowder. I'll give you some time to decide. What can I get you to drink?"

"I'll have a glass of Pinot Grigio," Alexis said.

"And you, sir?"

"I'll have a black whale, and if you could bring a pitcher of water, that would be great."

"Absolutely. I'll be right back."

Alexis leaned forward. "What's a black whale?"

"A Guinness poured over an Alaskan Amber."

Their drinks arrived and she watched Zeke's beer mix. The heavier beer cascaded into the lighter one, creating a tantalizing effect.

"That's really cool. How does it taste?"

He slid the glass over. "Try it."

Alexis licked her lips free of foam and he groaned inwardly. She was killing him. "You like it?"

"Really good. We should pick some up for our next popcorn night."

"Definitely."

He needed to change the subject quick to steer his mind toward something other than her mouth. "Was that the worst date you've been on?"

"Ha! No. Not by a long shot."

He had to know. "What was yours?"

"Your sister set me up on a blind date during our freshman year. She was dating an art student. Someone in her class." Alexis paused to take a sip of wine. "His brother was in the city, and she asked if I would double-date with them. I said sure. Since her date was a good-looking guy, his brother had to be decent, right?"

"He wasn't?"

She tipped her head. "Average."

"Okay, what was the problem?"

"Turned out he was a divorcé and pushing forty. I was nineteen."

"Sick."

Their food came, and the waitress asked if there was anything else.

"I'll have another glass of wine."

"Nothing for me. Thank you," Zeke said.

When the waitress left, he leaned forward. "What did you do?"

Alexis picked up her knife and buttered a slice of focaccia. "What could I do? I couldn't let Maggie go on the date alone with both guys."

He chuckled and broke a piece of bread. "How was it?"

"Totally creepy. Maggie had the sense to say we would meet them at the dance club. Her date complained a little, but she gave him her *look* and he backed down. We thought of not showing up, but we did."

"And . . ."

Alexis shrugged. "My date was by far the oldest guy there, and his eyes wandered over all the young asses. While I was dancing to a fast song with a group of others, he gyrated in front of me, and I almost lost it. I grabbed Maggie's hand and tugged her out of there. We laughed all the way home."

"Thanks for having her back."

"Of course. We always watched out for each other."

She went on to tell him about some of the other adventures she and Maggie shared in college, and before they knew it, the server was back to see if they wanted dessert. Zeke ordered a tiramisu to share.

He relaxed back in his chair. "How was your dinner?"

"I can see why this is your favorite place. The walleye was amazing. Even the side salad was above average. I liked the roasted beets and the citrus vinaigrette—delicious."

"We'll have to come back here again," Zeke said.

"Absolutely."

Their tiramisu arrived and they dug in. Alexis pulled her fork out of her mouth slowly and moaned. "This is to die for. A person could get drunk on all the coffee liqueur."

"I'm getting drunk watching you."

She laughed at him, but he truly was getting drunk on thoughts of Alexis.

"Your turn, Zeke. What was your worst date?"

Zeke set his fork down and pushed the plate toward Alexis. He'd enjoy the dessert more watching her eat it.

"That's easy. I met this girl at a bar."

"Of course you did."

"Hey, I don't meet all my dates at bars."

"Go on." She took another slow, sexy bite.

He cleared his throat and shifted in his chair. "We met at a small diner near Duluth, and she brought her brother with her."

"Let me guess, big burly dude with lots of overblown muscles to put you in your place."

"Umm, no. I think that would have been better. Her *little* brother. He was five years old."

"Oh. So, she couldn't find a babysitter?"

"I wish that was it." He paused for dramatic effect and sat forward. "She wanted to see how I acted around kids since she wanted a boatload and thought I'd make a great baby daddy."

"Nooo!" Alexis covered her mouth to stifle a laugh. "What did you do?"

"I threw a twenty-dollar bill on the table and got the hell out of there."

Alexis finished her wine. "As nice as this is, how about we head home. I have a few things to do before we start work tomorrow."

He left a generous tip in the leather folder and escorted Alexis to the truck. He pulled her door open, and she stopped and held his gaze before getting in. "Thanks for today. I had fun."

"How does this date rank?"

"Definitely a ten. Plus."

She stepped onto the running board before he could lean in and give her a kiss.

CHAPTER EIGHT

*A*lexis parked on Elmhurst Street, exited the warmth of her truck, buttoned her canvas jacket, and strapped on her tool belt. Susan had said she could find the key under the front mat. Not the best hiding place, but the neighborhood of older homes and mature trees had always been quiet. She'd put a lock box on the door this afternoon. She followed the sidewalk and took deep, calming breaths. The morning air was cool enough to see small puffs of steam as she exhaled.

The 1950s rambler with landscaped yard showed great potential. Although slightly overgrown, the mature oaks would provide much-needed shade on a hot summer day. A dog barked in the distance, and the call of a chickadee floated on the gentle breeze.

On first inspection, the wood casement windows looked to be original and would most likely need replacing. Alexis climbed the two cement steps, removed the key from under the mat, and unlocked the front entry. She pocketed the key. The heavy wooden door was in good shape, but they'd need a larger opening for better wheelchair access.

The only requirement of the competition she knew about so far was that both houses had to be accessible for people with disabilities. Her competitor's experience was mostly new construction, so she'd have a slight advantage. However, she knew Ryan Anderson built quality homes and would be a worthy opponent. Their sizable budget would allow both of them to create spectacular accommodations.

Alexis extended her measuring tape and made a note to expand the doorway and order vinyl windows. She stepped into the house. The air wasn't damp or musty, like some of her remodels; instead, the scent of citrus filled the air. The front door opened into a living room with wall-to-wall carpet on the floor. Although not in bad shape, she'd remove the broadloom. With her small crowbar in hand, she went to the wall and crouched down to pull back the floor covering. Happy to see original hardwood floors hiding underneath, Alexis hoped they spanned the entire room.

At the sound of a quick rap on the door, she stood.

Zeke walked in. "Sorry I'm late. My mom called on my way out the door. Owen and Maggie are buying the family home and property. She's excited at the offer Owen made, says it's beyond generous."

"That's wonderful. Maggie mentioned it earlier. She even hinted at starting a family."

Zeke nodded. "I really hope they get on it. I could use a few more nieces or nephews."

Alexis agreed. She was happy for Maggie and Owen but maybe a little envious too. She always thought she and Maggie would raise their children together. With limited time and options, she'd have to focus on being the best auntie ever.

Zeke cleared his throat. "Earth to Alexis."

"What?"

He took off his jacket and draped it over the kitchen counter. "Mom's moving to town and would like you to inspect the townhouse before she puts in an offer. One of the new builds on the lake. She said she'd feel better if you approved. I guess your opinion matters more than mine." He smiled, so he obviously hadn't taken offense.

"Did she say when?"

"She has an appointment with the realtor tomorrow afternoon. She'll give you a call."

"I'm happy to help." Alexis tapped a note on her phone for a reminder. Linnie was a lot like her own mom; she'd be anxious about the move. She'd meet with her to help calm her nerves and to listen to any apprehensions.

"Thanks." Zeke held out his hand. "Now, hand me your notebook and I'll take notes as we walk through the house."

With several pages filled with ideas on which walls to remove and what materials they needed, they exited the house into the backyard. *Great*. The crew of the other contest house had arrived to inspect their own project, which was situated directly behind the property where Alexis's crew would be working, the backyards separated by a four-foot chain-link fence.

Alexis shielded her eyes from the sun and focused on her task. "The roof and siding were replaced three years ago. We need to concentrate on the ramp and stairs before winter arrives. If my subcontractor has time, I'd like to extend the roofline and add a covered front porch. I'll contact him—"

"Alexis! Is that you?"

Ryan. Her stomach clenched at the sight of him. She might as well get the awkward first post-breakup meeting over with. "Well, I guess it's time for introductions," she mumbled to Zeke. She marched forward and Zeke followed, giving her the lead, which she appreciated.

"It's nice to see you again, Alexis. You look good." Ryan smiled.

Apparently, acting like they were old friends was what he was going with. The lack of guilt about his transgressions niggled at her. She would have liked to be in a loving relationship if she ever saw him again and instead here she was, face-to-face with her ex with no boyfriend and barely hanging on to her career. But he didn't need to know that.

"Thank you. I feel good." She stopped herself from fidgeting.

"James and Susan told me you were chosen for this contest," Ryan said.

"Yep . . . Ryan, this is my electrician and right-hand man, Zeke Reynolds." Zeke stood with his arms crossed and his feet spread wide.

"Nice to meet you, Zeke." Ryan turned his attention back to Alexis. "I won't be staying in town—"

A high-pitched laugh permeated the air, interrupting Ryan. Alexis clenched her fists as Raven sauntered over, her high-heeled leather boots aerating the ground. When she reached Ryan, she placed a hand on his shoulder. Her fingernails, inch-long daggers painted in black, reminded Alexis of a witch. "Wow, Alexis. It's been a long time."

"*Not long enough*," Alexis grumbled under her breath. "Raven."

Ryan spoke. "Raven will run the show for me here. But we'll see you tomorrow bright and early for the meeting, then I'll head back to the cities. When I'm back in town, let's have lunch."

Alexis's left brow hit her hairline, but she didn't answer. Ryan turned away and Raven followed in his wake.

"Over my dead body," Zeke grumbled. His hot breath against her ear made her heart pound. Always the protector. She liked when Zeke went all caveman.

CHAPTER NINE

The next day, they arrived early to hear the announcing of the contest rules. Alexis and Zeke met their demolition crew at the Elmhurst house. The rest of the team Alexis had assembled to work on the house would arrive tomorrow. "Thanks for coming," she said.

Alexis's demo crew lived to tear into walls, rip up floors, and destroy anything they could. They stood in front of her now like they did the first day of every job: crowbars and sledgehammers in hand, ready to pull the house apart.

"This house is in good shape, better than many of our remodels of late. The owners, Susan and James Henning, bought two houses to supply the Veterans' Center with extra housing for soldiers to use while they recover and transition." Some members of her crew were veterans themselves, and they nodded their approval.

"We have a half hour to walk through the house before meeting the owners in the backyard. We will be competing against a builder from the Twin Cities metro area, who will be working on the house behind us."

One of the crew members asked, "Why a competition?"

"Susan and James moved into the Whitmore Estate and will hire the crew who wins the competition to renovate their home."

Someone whistled.

Alexis nodded. "Both competition houses will be featured in *Remodeler's Platform* online magazine, so even if we don't win—which we will—we'll still gain some national exposure. I don't have to tell you what that kind of publicity would do for our town and our jobs."

"What's the timeline?" someone asked.

"That and the rest of the ground rules are what Susan and James will share with us this morning." Alexis checked her phone for the time. "The only thing I know is that the house will need to be accessible, so as we walk through, I'll point out the walls that need to come down. We'll reconvene after the contest rules are laid out and then get started on demo."

Alexis used her phone to film the rooms as they walked through the three-bedroom, two-bath rambler. She'd send the short video to Maggie so she could get started on choosing paint colors and furniture. Alexis opened the back patio door and stepped out onto the small deck. Her foot almost went through a rotted board. She turned and pointed. "Careful where you step." She glanced up at the gutters and made a mental note to have them cleaned out. She'd add seamless gutters to her wish list, a list she kept in case they had any leftover money.

They'd need to demo the small deck and build a new one before the first snowfall which, for their region, could be any day now. Luckily, snow wasn't forecasted for the next couple weeks, but they'd been surprised before and had a record snowfall last year. A mid-October blizzard had dumped ten inches on their small town. Hopefully the white stuff would hold off until the end of November.

Excited chatter came from the other house as they convened

in the backyard at the appointed time. The Hennings, along with Ryan, Raven, and their crew, made their way to the fence line.

Susan smiled and waved to Alexis while James shook hands with her and Zeke.

"Good morning!" Susan announced to the crowd. "My name is Susan Henning, and this is my husband, James." James balanced an expensive motion-picture type of camera on one shoulder and waved to everyone.

"He's filming?" Alexis said under her breath to Zeke, who stood next to her.

The corner of Zeke's mouth lifted into a grin. "Fun."

Susan stood before the two groups. "You may be wondering why James is filming. My husband's a retired documentary film-maker. Filming is in his blood. James will be documenting the renovations." Susan held up some papers. "I have releases for you all to sign. If you don't want to be on camera, please let us know. Having your every move documented is not for some, and is not a requirement of the contest."

Alexis glanced at her crew, who had gathered closer to hear. She didn't see anyone protesting. Being filmed wasn't her idea of fun, and she wondered if she could opt out.

"Okay, I'm sure you're all itching to get started," Susan said. "Here are the contest rules: Since these homes will be used for recovering veterans, they must be accessible and fully furnished. That's it. The rest is up to the individual crews to create a welcoming home for the people who will be staying here. I suspect it will be vets with families using these homes more often than individuals, so keep that in mind. Both places must be completed the week before Thanksgiving, giving you six weeks to finish the transformations."

The reality of the short six-week timeline hit Alexis like a hammer to a thumb. How would she get everything done in time and to the quality standards she needed to win the Whitmore bid?

Susan continued. "We have set up accounts for each of the contractors at the local lumberyard and hardware store, and I've set up an account at the furniture warehouse outside of town, so buy what you need. Each contractor will receive a prepaid credit card for purchases elsewhere. Let me stress, though, that we would like as many purchases as possible to come from local businesses. The reason we bought these homes is to give back to the community and support the veterans who served our country with their heroic sacrifices."

After a few questions were asked and answered, Susan rang a bell. "Let the games begin!" She chuckled. "I've always wanted to say that."

Both crews cheered and grunted like sports teams did when they broke apart after a time-out. They headed back to their respective houses, excited to demolish walls. Alexis rubbed her arms. The cool arctic breeze coming in from Canada chilled her to the bone.

The Hennings had arranged for the roll-off dumpsters, and they'd been delivered last night. Alexis grabbed the can of bright-orange spray paint from the kitchen counter. "Okay, guys, now that the rules are confirmed I'm going to put an X on the walls I want torn down. Save as much trim work as you can and set it aside. The cabinets aren't staying, but they're still in great shape. Be careful with them because they'll be donated. The small island comes out and isn't worth saving. Gut both bathrooms. You know the drill. I'll let you at it."

Her demo crew had worked for her on and off over the years, so she knew they didn't need supervision. She trusted them to work quickly and carefully and get the job done, including cleaning up before the end of the day.

THE NEXT MORNING, Zeke stood in the doorway and watched Alexis, wielding a crowbar, remove layers of linoleum from the kitchen floor. When James walked in holding his expensive-looking camera contraption, she kept her head down and tried to ignore him.

"Good morning!" James said. "Do you mind if I get started on filming?"

"Sure," Alexis said and went back to pulling up the linoleum.

James asked, "Can you explain what you are doing right now?"

Alexis opened her mouth then slowly closed it; she looked like a deer caught in the headlights.

Zeke cleared his throat, and James focused the shot on him instead. He smiled into the camera. "Zeke. Zeke Reynolds. Electrician and overall helper. Welcome to the Elmhurst house."

"The Elmhurst house?" James asked.

"Alexis always names the houses she renovates. Since this house is on Elmhurst Street, It's the Elmhurst house." He glanced back at Alexis, hoping she'd gotten over her sudden stage fright, but no, she had half the floor torn apart. "I've been working with Alexis for a long time. Renovation is really an art form, and Alexis Welby is a master carpenter." He smiled. "I have watched her turn run-down homes into amazing showpieces over the years." He turned to Alexis. "Remember that house that was infested with snakes?"

When Alexis only nodded, James lowered the camera and addressed Zeke. "Maybe this isn't a good time. I don't want to be in the way."

Zeke half-whispered, "Give us a second."

James nodded and pointed his camera elsewhere.

"Alexis? Do you have a minute?" Zeke motioned for her to follow him into the dining room adjacent to the kitchen.

With the public voting for the best house, it was important to create a sense of connection between the audience and the crew. They needed to deliver their A game when the camera rolled. He needed to figure out how to get Alexis to loosen up.

"WHAT's UP?" Alexis asked as innocently as she could muster. She didn't need Zeke to point out that she sucked in front of a camera. She always had.

The last time she'd been forced to perform in front of an audience was the production of *The Nutcracker Suite* in the fourth grade. She remembered it as if it were yesterday. She was cast as a Russian dancer. The night of the performance she'd been nervous, but her dad told her to focus on him the entire time she was onstage and to forget everyone else. She had done exactly as he suggested, and it had worked for a while. She and a dozen of her classmates were lined up across the stage with arms crossed, squatting and kicking their legs to the melodic music, when halfway through the dance, a classmate's dad stumbled into the auditorium, making a lot of noise and breaking her concentration. Her focus shifted from her father to the packed house. She grew so nervous she fell into the girl next to her, knocking her off-balance and making the entire line topple over like dominos. The parents chuckled, and by the time the dancers righted themselves, their song was over and they hurried offstage.

"What's going on in there?" Zeke asked. "You barely answered when James started filming."

She placed her hands on her hips. "I'm busy, I have work to do." She looked down at her scuffed-up work boots.

Zeke took her hands in his and ducked his chin to make eye contact. His thumbs massaged circles onto the backs of her hands. "Hey."

His touch calmed her nerves. She swallowed and tried to regain her composure.

"You are strong, independent, and a kick-ass contractor. Not to mention beautiful and smart as hell. You know more than all the guys working for you, and some of them have been at this a lot longer than you have."

She leveled him with a stare. "You don't understand. I've never done well in front of a camera."

"Then pretend it's not there."

"Yeah, easy for you to say. You're such a ham."

Growing up, Zeke had always loved the camera, his specialty being elaborate, acrobatic jumps into the lake.

His deep dimples made her stomach do flips. She closed her eyes and counted to ten, opening them again when Zeke spoke.

"I want you to go in there and show James what you're made of. Show him what this town and your friends see in you . . . what I see. Someone who knows her shit."

HOLDING Alexis's hands had Zeke wanting more. However, this wasn't the time or the place to confess his feelings. He looked down at their clasped hands and let go. He stuffed his hands into his front pockets. "Now, we're going to go back in there and I'm going to ask you some questions. I want you to focus on me and answer."

She took a deep breath. "Okay, let's do this."

James kept the camera trained on them as they walked back into the kitchen.

Zeke asked Alexis, "What are we working on today, boss?"

"Umm, we're tearing up the linoleum and . . . well, we're hoping, umm . . . to find hardwood floors below."

Alexis pointed to where she'd peeled back several layers of linoleum from the kitchen floor. "We've got some rot. We see this a lot in older homes. It looks like the ancient dishwasher had been leaking for a while."

Zeke walked to the area Alexis indicated. "How extensive do you think it is?"

"I'll need to replace the subfloor."

She swiped a lock of hair behind her ear. "Zeke, why don't you walk James through the house and explain the demo that happened yesterday. I'll continue the tear-up."

"Sure, yeah. No problem."

Zeke smiled at the camera. "Alexis is a little camera shy, but she doesn't shy away from hard work or from volunteering her time. She belongs to the revitalization committee here in Deer Creek Falls. This community is her home, and she wants it to thrive. Unfortunately, many homes and businesses have fallen into disrepair. It's the committee's mission to help bring the town back to its original glory. You'll notice, thanks to volunteers, there are baskets of flowers and banners lining Main Street. First impressions are important."

Zeke tripped over a stack of baseboards, lost his balance, and grabbed onto the temporary workbench. The sawhorse gave way on one side and knocked down a sheet of plywood and various tools. The sound was deafening in the empty house. He regained his balance and with a *ta-da*, straightened like he'd just landed a perfect dismount off the pommel horse. He should have been looking down instead of at the camera.

"Maybe don't use that part."

CHAPTER TEN

*W*ith a full thermos of coffee, Alexis headed for the Elmhurst house. The four hours' sleep she'd gotten each night over the past week was beginning to take its toll; hopefully the coffee would do the trick. The sun wouldn't appear for several hours. She yawned. With the noise ordinances, finishing the ramp outside would have to wait. For now, she'd concentrate on the kitchen. The hardwood floors throughout the rest of the house would be beautiful after her flooring guy sanded and sealed them, but unfortunately, after removing the linoleum, it had become clear that a few of the joists in the kitchen needed replacing. Maggie had chosen a new plank-style vinyl flooring Alexis would install this morning.

She drove up the asphalt driveway to the one-car garage. A concrete sidewalk led to the patio. The floodlight came on as she climbed the new deck. After they completed the ramp, the outside would fulfill the accessibility requirements of the contest.

She glanced around. The shades of the neighboring homes were drawn. She unlocked the door, pushed inside, and flipped on the lights. A few hours ago, she had finished laying a new subfloor so she could start installing the vinyl flooring. She tied one end of a chalk line to a nail and, holding the other, she snapped a line and got to work.

After getting a good chunk of the floor in place, Alexis stood and stretched. The sun could be seen on the horizon, and pinks and purples streaked the sky.

Zeke walked through the door, coffee in hand. "Don't you sleep anymore?"

"Good morning to you too," she said with a scowl. His adorable smile lit up his face. He looked like he'd slept great. She stuck out her tongue.

"Sorry, my bad. Good morning, sunshine."

Alexis walked over to her thermos and filled the cap full of lukewarm coffee. It would have to do. Not having had time to get a haircut, she could finally pull her hair into a stubby ponytail. She wondered how Maggie dealt with her long tresses every day. Alexis liked the simplicity of her short wash-and-go style.

Zeke set down his tool belt and held up a paper bag. Her mouth watered at the delicious savory smell. He unwrapped smoky bacon and egg sandwiches and placed them near the compound miter saw. Alexis's stomach grumbled. Loud.

"Apparently I'm hungry."

Zeke raised a brow. "I thought you might be."

He glanced out the kitchen window. "You've been working long hours."

"Yep." Alexis took a bite of her sandwich. "This is good. Thanks for breakfast."

"No problem. I figured you wouldn't have grabbed anything except coffee. Was I right?"

She crumpled up the wrapper. "I wanted to get an early start."

"The floor looks great. What time did you get here?"

"Around three, I guess." She shrugged like it wasn't a big deal. "I'll finish the floor and then head to the church. We have supplies being delivered today and I need to be there."

Zeke gathered up the wrappers and placed them into the trash, then walked over to her and placed his hands on her shoulders. "You're working too hard—we'll get it done. We're making great progress. Don't worry, and try to get more sleep."

Alexis breathed in Zeke's fresh scent. He had showered; the smell of his deep woodsy-musk shower gel teased her senses, and his damp hair begged for attention. She wanted to run her hands through it to tame it down. He stood too close, and she caught herself before reaching for him. She stepped back and Zeke's hands dropped to his sides.

"I'm concerned," he said.

"No need to be. I'm fine." Alexis shifted her feet, drawing up dust, and looked away. She was tired and wanted to cry, but she wouldn't. She was fine. She'd worked long hours before to hit deadlines. She cleared her throat. "Are you going to just stand there or are you going to help me finish this floor?"

"Let's do it."

Zeke didn't understand how much she had riding on this contest. No one, including Maggie, was aware of her financial situation. She'd never missed a deadline and she wouldn't start now. She couldn't let Kate Davis down either. She needed to finish the living space at the back of the old church before Kate arrived in town. Kate needed the space as living quarters as Alexis continued the renovations on the coffee shop. Although her crew had been split between the two jobs, she'd kept both on track. *So far.*

They finished the floor and covered it with cardboard. "Zeke, I'm heading to the church. Can you make sure the guys finish the ramp? I'll be back later. Maggie is picking up the paint for the walls and will be painting the bedrooms this afternoon."

"I've got it covered. Go."

She heard car doors slam, and they both went outside to greet the arriving crew.

WHEN ALEXIS ARRIVED at the church, her phone chimed with a reminder that she needed to meet Linnie at the townhome in a few hours to confirm whether it was a sound investment.

After she accepted the day's delivery, she got to work on staining the trim for the guest half bath, which didn't take much time at all. She then turned her attention to pulling an old heat register out of the floor, but when the ductwork released, it fell into the crawl space. *Crap.* She'd have to wait until Tommy got here after school. She looked at her watch as the side door opened. "Hey, Tommy. Perfect timing."

"Hey, boss. School let out early, some teacher thing." He smiled. "What do we have going on today?"

Alexis pointed to the opening in the floor. "The ductwork disconnected, and I need to thread it back into place. Can you stay up here while I head into the basement?"

"Are you sure you don't want me to crawl around down there? It's kind of creepy."

"Thanks, Tommy, but I don't know what I'll find. I may have to call HVAC if I can't fix it."

With flashlight in hand, Alexis pried open the old rickety door that led to the church cellar. She swallowed hard. The creak of the hinges reminded her of the endless horror films she and her girl-friends enjoyed watching in their youth. Give her an action or superhero film over horror any day. She never understood why young girls would run into a rundown barn or a haunted house with an ax- or chainsaw-wielding nutcase following them, leaving only one exit for themselves.

But here she was, entering a dark, damp cellar with dirt floors and only a single bare light bulb. At least there wasn't a madman after her.

Alexis switched on the light. It didn't even illuminate the

steep and narrow wooden steps. She'd have to ask Zeke to run a few more lights down here. She flicked on her black steel flashlight.

The dim and earthy space had low ceilings. At five foot ten, Alexis needed to crouch, straining her leg muscles. The confined space started to close in on her. She swung her flashlight in front of her to break up the thick cobwebs. Shivers radiated up and down her spine when she walked into a spiderweb. She dropped the flashlight and frantically wiped her face.

Maybe she should have called her HVAC guy, but they charged so much and she needed to stay on budget. Besides, she could reassemble ductwork. Easy peasy.

"Hey, boss. Can you hear me?"

She relaxed some when she heard Tommy's voice. He had to be lying on the floor, yelling through the vent.

"Almost there," she yelled.

Dammit. She'd have to crawl on her belly, soldier style, to reach it. She'd brought the wrong flashlight; she needed a penlight she could hold between her teeth, or a head lamp. She looked around for a place she could prop up the flashlight to direct the beam of light.

"Hey, Tommy. Can you shine a light down here?"

"Sure, give me a minute."

Alexis heard him walk overhead to find a flashlight and return.

"Okay, how's this?"

"Great. Just hold it like that."

She unhooked her tool belt, pushed it forward, and belly-crawled over the dirt. Thank goodness she'd worn gloves. The light illuminated several sets of mouse bones. *Shit.* She hated mice, even dead ones. She cringed. With her gloved hand, she swiped them out of her way.

Alexis continued to belly-crawl. There was no way to turn

around; she'd have to back up when she was done. She felt the damp earth rub against her skin. She closed her eyes and centered her thoughts. Next time, she'd pay someone to do this. No matter the cost.

She reached the ductwork where it had detached. With just enough space to roll onto her back, she connected the round aluminum duct pipe and moved it back into place. She reached for the screwdriver she had placed in her back pocket and tightened the clamp. "Okay, Tommy, screw it in place so I can get out of here."

Now with only her beam of light attached to the rafter, she needed to crawl out.

Tommy's muffled voice came through the floor. "Good to go, boss."

She flipped back over to her stomach, her shoulder touching the floor joists, and inched her way out.

Alexis looked down at her dirt-covered clothes. Her hair needed washing, and she knew if she didn't run home now, she wouldn't have time to shower before meeting Linnie.

"I need to head out. You can knock off for the day as well. Thanks for sticking around, Tommy, I really appreciate it. Sean will be back to work on Monday."

"It was sad to hear about his mom. See you tomorrow?"

Sean's mom had been in a nursing home the next town over, but she had passed. He had called and let Alexis know he'd be back to work next week after his mom's graveside service.

"You'll see me at some point, but I'm sending Zeke over in the morning. Call me if you need anything."

"Will do."

Alexis brushed the cobwebs and dirt from her clothing and headed for home. She sent a quick text to Zeke: *I'm meeting up with your mom. I just finished crawling around in dirt, spiders, and mouse bones. I'll need to use your shower.*

I'll be right home, he responded.

In your dreams, Reynolds.

Zeke sent a wink emoji and her face flushed. She sent another text: *I'll head back to the Elmhurst when I'm finished with your mom.*

I'll be here. Good luck with Mom. Tell her to buy the place.

Alexis smiled at his reply. Zeke didn't understand that the reason his mom was hesitant about purchasing the townhome wasn't because she needed an inspection, but because moving out of the home she raised her family in would be hard. Linnie was Alexis's second mom, and if she could be some comfort to her, she was happy to meet, inspect, and reassure her she was making the right decision. Besides, Linnie would spend time at the family home when Maggie and Owen continued the tradition of Saturday-night dinners, and fill in running the resort when they were out of town.

She texted Zeke back. *I will. I'll fill you in later.*

CHAPTER ELEVEN

With four weeks left and her foreman still out on paternity leave, Alexis's muscles ached with exhaustion. She removed her tool belt and draped it over the end of the sawhorse. Twelve-hour days, six days a week, were taking their toll. She needed a long soak in the hot tub to soothe her tired body, and an early bedtime.

Her crew chief, Evan, walked into the kitchen. "We're making great progress. Any word on your former foreman—Pete, right?"

"Yes, but he hasn't gotten back to me yet." She was happy with the progress on the Elmhurst house, but she worried that if Pete couldn't help her out, she'd fall behind schedule.

"Are we calling it a day, boss?" asked Evan.

Alexis leaned against the newly added support that helped to bear the weight of the open floor plan. "Yep. I think we all deserve to knock off at a decent hour and enjoy the rest of our weekend."

Zeke came through the back door with a smile on his face, rubbing his hands together. "So, who's joining me at Oktoberfest tonight? Garrett will have samples of his new brew, and the firehouse is hosting a s'mores station by the lake, behind the lodge."

The rest of the crew joined them, chattering about heading to the festival, some of their wives already there. "Count me out," Alexis said.

"Come on, Alexis. You can make time for one drink, and I know how much you like s'mores. Think of the silky milk chocolate and gooey marshmallow sandwiched between crisp honey graham crackers." Zeke's mouth twitched into a smirk.

He was playing hardball. Zeke knew once she visualized any dessert, she couldn't banish it from her mind.

He continued, "My family will be there and so will the Reid family. Plus, Maggie made me promise to talk you into coming. You said it yourself, and I quote: 'We all deserve to enjoy our weekend.' Come relax by the lake."

She hated when Zeke threw her own words back at her, especially when he followed up with a flash of that deep dimple and a panty-melting grin she had a hard time resisting.

Maybe it wouldn't hurt to take a break, but she needed to shower and change clothes before heading over. She hoped her hot water heater arrived soon; she was sick of not having her own shower. Her crew might not feel the need to clean up, but she wouldn't think of showing up in her work clothes, smelling like sawdust and sweat. No way.

With a tired sigh, she caved. "Sure. I need to freshen up. I'll meet you there," she said to Zeke. They both knew very well she'd be at his house showering, but she didn't need her crew to find out.

"Maggie put me in charge of dragging you out tonight. I'll stop by in an hour, and we can walk over together."

"Fine," Alexis said. Thank God she'd found two more able-bodied men to work the Elmhurst house. Maybe she could relax tonight.

"Rest up, everyone, and enjoy your day off tomorrow. I'll see you all bright and early Monday morning." Alexis shrugged on her coat. "Let's go, Zeke, before I change my mind."

COMFORT WON out as Alexis pulled on a long dark-gray turtleneck sweater and black leggings. She paired her outfit with her knee-high leather boots and her latest Chloe creation, a long hammered-steel necklace she'd bought at Rural Chic Boutique.

She finger-combed her chin-length bob and added some mousse for a messy but stylish look. Maggie had dragged her offsite the other day for the last appointment at the salon. She appreciated Maggie for taking care of her when she'd most likely have kept putting off getting her hair done.

"Hey, Alexis. You about ready?" Zeke called from the kitchen.

She stepped into the room, and he whistled. "Gorgeous."

Alexis's face flushed from the compliment. Zeke complimented females all the time, but this time she had the strange feeling his admiration and the seductive pull of his mouth meant more.

"Thanks." She grabbed her boots and pulled them on while Zeke watched. She had noticed slight changes in his behavior toward her. Could she chance their friendship by making a move, or would she embarrass herself if she'd misread the compliments as more? The way his T-shirt showed off his sculpted, muscular shoulders had her entertaining the thought of sliding her hands over his body.

She averted her eyes when his grin ticked up. "I'm ready," she said. She tucked her cash and license into a small cross-body purse. She needed to cool her thoughts and her body down.

Zeke held the door open. "Ethan texted me and said there are several food trucks lined up in front of the lodge."

"Then by all means, let's hurry. I'm starving. Plus, I need one of those *gooey* s'mores."

"Too much of a visualization?" He laughed.

"You know me too well."

She was surprised to see how many people had flocked to Oktoberfest. She hardly ever went, being in such a hurry every fall to finish jobs requiring outside work before winter came. Blustering cold winds and piles of snow weren't her favorite working conditions.

They approached Main Street. "Wow," she said. "It's a good thing we walked. There isn't a place to park anywhere. It's nice to see a lot of people in town. The turnout is almost as good as Labor Day." Alexis's stomach growled as she inhaled the smoky aroma of barbeque.

"Come on." Zeke grabbed her hand, and they jogged across the street in front of the Deer Creek Lodge. When they reached the food trucks, she noticed he hadn't surrendered her hand. At the low, guttural purr of a motorcycle, she turned to look. She knew that bike. A 2003 Harley-Davidson Heritage Softail.

The motorcycle pulled to the curb and the rider took off his helmet. "Hey, sexy lady, need a ride?"

Zeke tightened his grip on her hand. "Ignore him, Alexis."

CHAPTER TWELVE

*Z*eke's hand fell to his side as Alexis released it, her smile widening. "Pete?"

The rider, a tall, muscular man clad in leather, dismounted with a huge grin and strolled toward her. "Yep, it's me, General."

Alexis ran to him and jumped into his arms. He twirled her around and set her down.

She smacked him on the arm. "I can't believe it's you. When I didn't hear from you, I figured you were off doing God knows what."

Zeke's disappointment at the way Alexis greeted this man made him regret he hadn't acted on his feelings sooner. He walked closer to get a read on Pete and on why Alexis would be so friendly with a former coworker. Didn't a hug suffice? Only in Zeke's dreams had she jumped into his arms like that.

"As soon as I got your message, I filled my truck with tools, strapped down the bike, and headed north. I'd never pass up a chance to work for you again." Pete kissed Alexis's temple.

"It's so good to see you! I missed you," she said.

Zeke cleared his throat to break up the reunion. Pete looked at him over Alexis's shoulder.

"General, I didn't know you had a boyfriend. He looks like he wants to chop me to bits and feed me to the fishes." His mouth curled up into a shit-eating grin that Zeke wanted to wipe off his face. Alexis laughed.

Pete was right; he wasn't happy.

Alexis spoke up. "Pete, this is my *friend*—not boyfriend—Zeke Reynolds, who's also my electrician."

Did she really have to emphasize their status?

Pete stepped forward and offered his hand. "Nice to meet you, Zeke. You must be Maggie's brother. I just booked a cabin for a few months at your sister's place." Pete stowed his helmet on his bike.

"General, huh? I haven't heard that nickname before," Zeke muttered.

"Yeah, well, it's my nickname for Alexis. She was my General Contractor on a jobsite in the cities. The name stuck." Pete snaked an arm around her shoulder and pulled her close.

Zeke knew he needed to be civil to the guy; he'd clearly dropped everything to help Alexis. "Thanks for coming, Pete."

"No problem. I hope I didn't interrupt anything. Your grandma is a real hoot—told me all about Oktoberfest going on in town, and that Maggie was already here. I figured Alexis would be with Maggie."

Addressing Alexis again, he said, "I texted you when I got into town, but figured you were on the jobsite."

Alexis pulled out her phone. "I'm sorry, obviously I haven't checked my messages in a while."

"Why don't you join us, Pete? We'll introduce you to our family and friends."

"Sounds good, thanks." Pete held out his arm for Alexis to take. "I'm all yours, General."

Alexis interlaced her arm with Pete's and cuddled into his leather jacket, which Zeke didn't like. He wanted to take her back to his place and show her what she meant to him. Instead, he followed close behind and faked a smile when needed.

Zeke observed how friendly Alexis and Pete were. It was as if Pete were her favorite candy she couldn't get enough of. He wondered if there had ever been anything sexual between them, or if she contained Pete to a box like she had been doing with him.

"People around here only know me as Alexis. So, cool it with 'General.' I don't need a nickname."

"Yes, ma'am."

Zeke didn't know what to think of Pete. He wanted to like the guy, but he didn't like how close he and Alexis were. *Hell.* He was jealous. Alexis always made a point not to date her employees—which didn't sit well, at least not anymore, because he was her employee. He'd make it his mission to find out if she and Pete were more than friends. Working closely with Alexis the past few weeks had him wanting more. He wanted to use his hands to explore every inch of her body. He wanted to kiss her minty breath and inhale her citrusy scent. To be her favorite candy to indulge in.

The ongoing banter between Pete and Alexis interrupted his thoughts. They stepped in line at the Smoky Bob's Barbeque food truck. "You guys order, my treat," Zeke said, trying to take the upper hand.

"You don't have to do that, Reynolds," Pete countered.

"You drove all the way here to help Alexis. We really appreciate it."

Alexis confirmed, "We do, Pete. We appreciate you coming on such short notice. We've been running between jobsites for the last two weeks. And Zeke, you're not buying. This meal is on me. Order as much as you like." They approached the window and ordered their meals. Zeke chose two mouthwatering brisket sandwiches with crispy onions, and Pete ordered the brisket tacos.

Zeke smiled when Alexis ordered the loaded brisket salad; she always made sure to eat her vegetables.

Alexis paid, slipped a tip into the jar, and said, "Let's head lakeside. Maggie texted and said they have a table saved."

"I heard she got married," Pete said before taking a bite of his taco.

Zeke and Alexis nodded.

"He's a former SEAL, so no flirting, Pete. I don't want to see him kick your ass," Alexis admonished.

Pete faked innocence. "Who, me?"

"Between you and Zeke, I don't know who'd get the biggest flirt award." Alexis caught sight of the Reynolds family; they'd pushed two picnic tables together. She nodded to them.

A joyful scream filled the evening festivities as Maggie bolted out of her seat when she saw Pete.

"This should be good." Zeke smirked.

Alexis grinned at Maggie's exuberance. "Just so you know, there wasn't ever anything between Pete and your sister."

"Good to know." Zeke felt a little better but noticed Alexis didn't mention if there had ever been anything between *her* and Pete. Owen was mid-chew when his wife bolted from her seat and ran to Pete, wrapping him in a hug. Zeke smiled because his own face had probably held the same stunned expression as Owen's when Alexis ran into Pete's arms moments ago. Except Maggie was Owen's wife, and Zeke didn't have any claim on Alexis. The queasy feeling in his gut about possibly losing Alexis to someone else had him rethinking when he'd finally voice his feelings for her.

Zeke walked over to his brother-in-law and placed a hand on his shoulder. "They worked together in the cities. Nothing more. She's just happy to see him."

"What do you know about him?" Owen asked as he wiped his face and stood.

"No more than what Alexis shared minutes ago."

"Hmm."

Maggie walked Pete over and introduced him to her husband. "Owen, this is my friend Pete Larson. Pete worked with Alexis on several jobs and helped us gut some historic homes. Pete, this is the love of my life, my husband, Owen Jacobs." Maggie beamed.

Pete set his food on the table and shook Owen's hand. "Nice to meet you."

"You too." Owen signaled to the table. "Join us."

Zeke settled alongside Alexis and across from Paige and Ethan. Alexis introduced Pete to everyone and announced he'd be taking over the renovation of the church / coffee shop's living quarters for the new owner. Zeke noticed how Alexis's shoulders had relaxed. If Pete could help Alexis breathe easier and get more sleep, he'd welcome his help and play nice. For now.

THEY'D ALL EATEN and moved to one of several fire pits to enjoy s'mores. Alexis stood and stretched after stuffing herself until she couldn't breathe. "Pete, do you have plans tomorrow? I'd like to meet with you at the jobsite and give you the rundown."

"Sounds like a plan, Gen—Alexis. Have you gotten your bike restored yet? I thought before storing mine for the winter, we could cruise around the lakes, head farther north maybe, take a short road trip. What do you think?"

Alexis, giddy at the idea of being on a bike again, jumped at the chance. "Haven't had time, but I'd love to ride. It's been too long. So yes, but on one condition: I get to sleep in."

Maggie snorted. "She should be ready by six then."

"How about eight o'clock," Alexis suggested. "I'll text you my address."

Owen spoke up. "We have room in the garage at the main house if you'd like to store your bike while you're here. You probably won't be getting much time to ride before the snow falls."

"Thanks, Owen, I appreciate that."

Alexis addressed the Reynolds clan. "I need to crawl into bed. Enjoy your evening."

Zeke stood. "I'm calling it a night too. It's been a long week. I'll walk you home." They made the rounds and said their good-byes. Zeke ruffled his twin nieces' hair and ducked out of the way before he was smacked. At ten, they were at an age where their hair mattered to them.

The evening had cooled into the low fifties, but the breeze remained gentle, carrying the aroma of scrumptious food, teasing Alexis's senses even though she couldn't eat another bite.

"What do you think of Pete?" she asked Zeke as they walked back to their respective homes.

"He seems like a nice guy. Were you two ever an item?"

She laughed. "Why? Jealous?"

Zeke shrugged. "Yeah, I guess I am."

Alexis stopped walking. He turned to her. They were under a large sugar maple that was slowly losing its leaves, standing in its colorful remnants. Zeke held her gaze, their faces close. She wasn't sure what was about to happen. Did she want Zeke to kiss her? Definitely. But was it wise? Definitely not.

Zeke reached for her, cupped her face with both hands, leaned in . . . and then the neighbor's chocolate lab jumped on them and barked.

Alexis shrieked.

"Shit." Zeke stepped back and ran his hand through his hair.

"Hi, you two!" Their neighbor reached them and hooked the leash back onto her dog's collar. "Sorry to interrupt." She smiled and tugged her dog away. "Carry on."

Yeah, right. Thanks a lot. Alexis watched the turmoil on Zeke's face. He reached for her hand and gave it a soft squeeze, encouraging her to come with him. Alexis was ready to drag him into her bedroom, her girly parts reacting to the possibilities.

They walked around to the back door of her house in silence, neither one of them knowing what to say. If it weren't for the exuberant dog, they'd be wrapped up in each other's arms, tasting and exploring each other.

Her heart raced with anticipation when he stepped close and skimmed his thumb over her cheek.

"Good night, Alexis." Zeke kissed her on the forehead. "Sweet dreams."

Alexis stood transfixed as he retreated through the gate. Sweet dreams? Ha! Dreams about Zeke wouldn't be sweet but sizzling hot.

ZEKE, tangled in his bedsheets, woke with thoughts of Alexis beside him. All he'd wanted to do was kiss her last night and profess his feelings, but he wasn't sure he should pursue her now that Pete had arrived. She'd only think he was jealous and making a move solely because Pete was in town. He was a dumbass for not kissing her before last night. Now he needed to make damn sure she wanted him and not Pete.

At the rumble of a motorcycle, he reached for his jeans. He made it to the front window in time to see Alexis straddle the bike and wrap her arms around Pete. Zeke ran his fingers through his bed-tousled hair and headed into the kitchen. His plan had been to relax on his day off, but he felt restless and needed to do something constructive.

He sent a text to Ethan. *Mind if I use your gym this morning?*

Ethan responded right away: *Go on over. Paige is helping Mom and I'm helping Abe. You know where the key is.*

Pumping iron should keep his mind focused instead of thinking about Alexis's body pressed up against another man.

~

STILL RESTLESS AFTER A GRUELING WORKOUT, Zeke stopped in at his mom's new place, thinking he could help her unpack a few boxes.

She greeted him with a hug. "Paige just left. Did you come to help?"

"Yep. With whatever you need." He glanced around at her new digs and the way her furniture fit perfectly in the space. Alexis had convinced her the townhome was just right, and he agreed. His mom seemed happy.

After a few hours of unpacking and organizing, Zeke pulled his phone from his back pocket. He didn't know why he expected Alexis to text him. Being inseparable the last two weeks had messed with his sanity. Being with Alexis brought the best out of him. He no longer had the need to flirt or to think of anyone but his sexy contractor. The problem was, she wasn't his, and he'd need to accept it or do something to rectify the situation.

"Honey, are you expecting a call?"

He'd been deep in thought, and his mom's voice startled him. "Nope, just checking my email," he lied.

"Come on. Let's visit the diner for an early dinner. I don't have anything in the house."

"Sure. I could eat."

~

ROSIE GATHERED two menus and gestured toward a back booth. Zeke liked mom time and was happy to accompany her to dinner.

83

"The special is a hot beef sandwich or walleye with glazed carrots and garlic mashed potatoes."

Linnie handed the menu back after taking a quick peek. "The hot beef sounds delicious, Rosie. Thank you."

"Make that two." Zeke winked at Rosie and handed her the menu.

"Anything else to drink besides water?"

"Coffee. Decaf for me," Linnie said.

"I'm fine with water. Thanks."

"Coming right up."

Excited over the move, Linnie beamed. "It's nice to be close to the lake without all the work. And the other wonderful thing . . ." She leaned forward and spoke in a whisper.

Zeke's jaw dropped when his mom confessed, in a hushed tone, how much Owen had paid for their family home. Happy for her, he hoped she'd do some traveling with her good friend Patricia, Alexis's mom. They'd been talking about taking a trip together for years. With less responsibility, she just might.

Their dinners arrived and they dug in.

His phone chimed, and he pulled it from his back pocket. *Rain starting in ten minutes.* He rolled his eyes and placed the phone facedown on the table. He had hoped it was Alexis saying she had gotten back with a "Hey, stop by." No such luck.

Zeke pushed the mashed potatoes around on his plate.

"A penny for your thoughts."

He glanced up at his mom. "It's nothing."

"Is it about Alexis and her visitor?"

He took a sip of his water. "I'd rather not talk about it."

She sighed and placed her fork on the table, pushed her plate to the side, and leaned forward. "This is your chance to tell Alexis how you feel. You might have been in different places before, but I think . . . This could possibly be the time. Give it a shot. I need grandbabies."

"Don't worry, Ethan and Maggie will supply you with some."

She sighed at the pleasant thought.

Thankful that the diner wasn't busy and that they were seated away from the only two other families enjoying their meals, he leaned forward and lowered his voice. "I don't want to mess things up. She's under a lot of pressure with this contest and winning the bid for the Whitmore Estate. I don't want to be a distraction. What if she doesn't feel the same?"

"What if she does?" His mom placed her hand on his. "Zeke, you two have been denying your feelings for too long. Don't think the women of this town haven't noticed. The dance you shared the night of your sister's wedding . . . Let's just say that when you left, Alexis looked like someone kicked her puppy."

His smile picked up momentum as his mother continued.

"She looks at you like you're a gooey dessert," she said with a laugh. "Don't take the word of an old lady. Talk to Maggie if you need reassurance. She knows Alexis better than anyone."

AFTER DROPPING his mom off at home, Zeke pulled into his driveway. No sign of Pete's bike. He threw his keys on the kitchen counter and grabbed a beer from the fridge. He'd walk next door to see if Alexis was home.

When he stepped into his backyard, he heard Alexis's favorite eighties station. He opened the gate connecting their backyards. Pete and Alexis were in her hot tub.

"Hey, Zeke. Join us," Pete called.

Too late to turn back, Zeke closed the gate and walked up to the patio. "How was your tour of the lakes?"

"Oh man, it was awesome. We visited Itasca State Park where the Mississippi River starts, hiked some, and stopped at a few interesting shops. Not a lot of places open on Sunday."

"Join us, Zeke," Alexis said.

Zeke's phone rang. "One sec, it's Ethan." He turned his back on the happy couple. His brother had perfect timing. "What's up?"

"Nick and Cole are on their way over for a bonfire. Thought you might like to join us."

"I'll be there shortly." Zeke hung up and sent a prayer of thanks to the gods for rescuing him from an awkward situation.

"Everything okay?" Alexis asked.

He finished his beer in one swig, and his eyes trailed over Alexis in her pink camo bikini. "Yep. I'll see you tomorrow." He turned and hightailed it out of there.

CHAPTER THIRTEEN

*Z*eke's smile grew when he saw Roman standing by the bonfire next to Ethan. Their oldest brother didn't have a lot of free time between raising preteen daughters and running what had once been their parents' landscaping business, Reynolds and Sons. Zeke had a lot of respect for him—after all, Roman had been the one to hold the family together after their dad passed when they were barely out of their teens—and hoped he'd find someone to share his life with. Hell, only one of his brothers had lucked out in that department. "Where are my beautiful nieces tonight?" he asked.

"Hey, little brother." Roman awarded him with a one-arm hug. "They're with Owen and Maggie. Maggie owed me some *girl time*." He emphasized with air quotes. "The girls don't like when I call it babysitting, because they're not babies anymore."

"Ha! They gotcha there."

Roman responded with a grunt.

Nick and Cole pulled into the drive. Ethan's security light could illuminate a ball field, and Zeke shielded his eyes with one hand as they made their way down to the lake. Cole set a cooler on one of the bench seats.

They exchanged greetings and Cole passed around beverages. "Garrett couldn't make it but sent beer with us. I have to say, having a brother who owns a brewery is definitely a perk."

"I second that," Nick said and turned his attention to Zeke. "I heard you had some trouble in LA."

Always to the point, Nick had a quiet but serious demeanor. He made a great interim sheriff for their small town. He and Roman were a lot alike; they were both the eldest sons of a large family, and they wore that responsibility like a badge of honor.

"Minor bruising," Zeke said with a shrug and grabbed the nearest stick to stir the fire.

"GSW to your upper arm is what I heard."

"Just a graze."

"I heard Mandy Blake had her legs wrapped around you." Cole snickered.

"Well, technically that's true, but it's not what you think. More like a painful and gyrating hug."

The guys all broke into laughter and Zeke rolled his eyes. It was the thought of Alexis wrapped around him that kept him up at night. He had a reputation as a flirt, but what the guys didn't know was that he flirted to make women feel good about themselves. Not that it hadn't gotten him what he wanted a time or two.

Roman knocked shoulders with him when all the guys had quieted down. "What's going on with you?"

Zeke threw the stick on the ground and raked his free hand through his hair. "I don't know. In a funk, I guess."

"Oh hell, Zeke, just admit it already," Ethan said.

"What?"

Roman poked at the fire, moving a log around. "You've been harboring feelings for Alexis Welby ever since you moved back home."

"Hell, I thought there was something going on with you two when you were teenagers," Cole said.

"We were friends, that's it." Zeke was attracted to Alexis back when she and her mom stayed at the resort during the summers, but as a teenage boy, he was attracted to any girl wearing a bikini. Back then, they *were* only friends.

He started to regret coming to hang out with the guys. They were as bad as the busybodies in town. "What we don't get is why you haven't made your move. You flirt with everyone, yet you don't acknowledge your feelings toward Alexis," Cole said.

"I'm surprised Grandma hasn't set things in motion for you two," Ethan said. "Maybe you should have a talk with her. I'm sure she'd be happy to help you out—heck, she helped me."

Nick chuckled and said, "Life's too short. I think we all have regrets. I know I do. Don't let her get away, because the right woman will move on with or without you."

Zeke let Nick's words sink in. He'd never known Nick to open up, and the rest of the guys seemed just as stunned when he looked around at everyone else. "Do you think she knows how I feel? Because apparently I haven't fooled any of you."

Nick slapped him on the back. "Nope. That's why you need to make a move."

Zeke rested his arms on his legs. "I almost kissed her."

Ethan had just taken a drink and almost spit it out in shock. "Okay. Almost? The funk you're in right now tells me that was your first mistake." He shook his head.

"I'm giving her time."

"And . . ." the guys all said in unison.

"You guys are a bunch of gossips. *And* she is currently sitting in her hot tub with Pete after spending the day pressed up against him on the back of his bike."

Roman sat down on the bench. "I think we're going to be here awhile."

ALMOST MIDNIGHT, and with a long day tomorrow, Zeke said his goodbyes and hauled his ass back home. He knew what he needed to do. He'd wake Alexis up if he had to, or haul Pete out of the hot tub. Talking with the guys tonight put his dating life into perspective. No wonder she didn't act on his advances. Well, until last night . . . but then he'd shut it down. Stupid.

Zeke pulled into his garage but kept the door open to haul out a few tools from the bed of his truck. He smelled of wood and smoke, the one thing about bonfires he didn't like, but put up with. He loved his quiet neighborhood. Everyone asleep for the night. He enjoyed late nights and early mornings the most.

He glanced over at Alexis's dark house. She'd hate him for waking her up, since she didn't sleep as much as she should, so he put his tools away and went inside.

He crawled into bed and sent Alexis a text. *Are you awake?*

He fell asleep waiting for a reply.

ALEXIS HAD MISSED a text from Zeke last night. She had left her phone in the kitchen to charge. She started the coffeemaker, pulled out a thermos, and sent a quick text to Zeke even though she'd see him in a few minutes: *Sorry I didn't see your text last night. Did something happen at the house?*

Zeke replied, *All good at the house. Only wanted to see if you were still up.*

She wished she hadn't been sleeping so she could ask him why he took off so fast. *I'm leaving now, talk soon?*

Yep. See you soon.

Alexis shoved her keys into her pocket, filled her thermos,

and walked out the door. Something was amiss. Zeke had never texted her in the middle of the night. She'd find out soon.

On the way to work, Lily called to set up her third blind date. Alexis was going to be glad when the dating agreement was done. Lily promised Josh was different from her last two dates and she'd have fun. Alexis hoped so.

The delivery truck had just dropped off the windows when she arrived at the Elmhurst house. They had been on back order, but now they'd finally be able to set them and patch the siding. It might be see-your-breath chilly, but it wasn't snowing. She waded through the inventory. "These aren't our windows," she said to anyone who was listening. Zeke was speaking to someone on his phone, and he held up a hand for her to wait a minute.

He finished his call and walked over with an invoice in hand. "Hey, Alexis. They delivered our windows to Ryan's house. The lumberyard said the invoice had the wrong address. It'll be a couple hours before the truck can get there to pick them up."

"That doesn't make sense. I placed the order myself. We can't wait for the truck to come back. Let's go get as many as we can."

"I've already called in reinforcements."

"Really?"

"That's what I'm here for," Zeke said.

"Well yeah, and for my viewing pleasure." Alexis's hand flew to her mouth. She blamed little sleep and waking up from a sensual dream of Zeke.

His eyes twinkled with mischief. He reached for her wrist and pulled her close. "Feel free to look . . . *and touch*." With his other hand, he traced her jawline and tipped her chin. With their lips close, she inhaled his woodsy scent. She closed her eyes as Zeke leaned in, her body radiating with desire.

The shuffle of feet sounded from behind them and they flew apart. *Shit.* She was acting careless on the jobsite.

"Did I interrupt something?" Maggie asked. "I'd like to go

over the paint colors and a few lighting choices I brought with me if you have time, but I *could* come back."

Alexis cleared her throat. "Zeke was helping me with an unruly eyelash. Let's see those paint colors."

That was close.

WITH A PLAN for painting and hanging lights at the Elmhurst house, Alexis headed to the church. "Wow, Pete, this kitchen is amazing. Kate will be pleased." Alexis ran her hands over the white granite countertops. She always loved when the kitchen cabinets and countertops were in, because it made it seem they'd made a lot of progress, the end in sight.

"The tile arrived a few hours ago." Pete stepped around her and motioned to the boxes. "Stan will be here to install the kitchen and bathroom floors tomorrow."

"Perfect." Her phone rang and she glanced at the caller. "It's my plumber."

Pete walked away to give her privacy, and she found him again when she'd finished her call.

"I'm going to head home," she told him. "My plumber needs to get in to install my new water heater. Call me if you need anything."

"Will do, General."

Alexis sent a quick text to Zeke: *I'm heading home. My water heater is being replaced, and I have an interview with James.*

Go get 'em, tiger. A kiss emoji followed Zeke's text.

Not knowing how to respond, she headed home with a huge smile on her face. She didn't bother telling him about her date tonight.

CHAPTER FOURTEEN

With her new water heater installed, Alexis took a shower and got ready for the interview with James. She poured herself a glass of water to help with her dry throat. She'd put him off long enough. He'd be here any minute.

When the doorbell rang, she placed her water glass on the counter and checked her hair in the entryway mirror before opening the door. "Hi, James. Come on in."

"Thanks for having me to your house, Alexis. I thought it would be quieter, with fewer distractions. Where would you like me to set up?" He glanced around her living room.

She ushered him through the house. "Either at the dining room table or in the living room is fine."

He nodded. "The living room has good light."

She moved out of the way as James placed his camera on a tripod.

"Where would you like me to sit?" she asked.

James pointed to the couch. "I'll take the chair. Just look at me and act like the camera isn't there."

Alexis blew out a breath. "Okay. I can do that."

They sat. "What made you want to become a carpenter? Sorry, *contractor*," he corrected himself.

"Can I walk over to the fireplace?"

"Sure, let me grab the camera."

Great. She was already flubbing up the interview because she couldn't sit still. She got up, walked to the fireplace, and picked up the picture of her and her dad posing with their tool belts around their waists. They stood in front of the tree fort they'd built together. Her young self smiled widely for the camera, the heavy tool belt sinking low over her skinny hips. "My dad."

James focused the camera on the photograph.

She cleared her throat of emotion. "My dad, Sergeant Steven Welby, served in the Army. When he was on leave the summer I turned twelve, we built this tree fort. He died a year later." She swallowed hard and stared at the picture in her hand. "I cherish the time we spent together. From that day forward I wanted to build things. With the work I do now on old homes, I'm giving them a second chance. A chance I never had with my dad. I remember him being patient and paying attention to details. He took great pride in everything he did." She placed the picture back in its place on the mantel, running her fingers over the frame.

"Mom and I had to leave the house after my dad died, and on moving day, I went to the backyard and got something to take with me." She walked over to the entry room wall and pointed to a framed board. "We carved this wood sign with our initials." The sign read KEEP OUT in large, bold letters.

"Nice," James said and nodded. He cleared his throat. "Life is about the memories you make. And that's why I'm a documentary filmmaker. Sharing memories and experiences has always been my mission."

"It sounds like our goals are similar," she said.

He nodded and placed his camera on the tripod across from Alexis. They settled back into their seats, opposite each other.

"Would you say remodeling is your passion? Or do you also build new?"

Alexis thought a moment. "I've built new homes and additions, but I love renovating. There's plenty of people who build homes and cabins around the lakes up here and the area has expanded in the last decade, so there will always be a need for new construction, but I specialize in making the old, new again. There's a vibe, an energy that old homes give off that new homes don't. Don't get me wrong, new homes will create memories, but the old ones . . . their stories can continue."

"You do a lot for this town, don't you?"

"I like to be involved."

"One of the things I admire about this community is the revitalization committee," James said.

"Yes. The townspeople take a lot of pride in their community. Our former mayor Elsie Andrews started the revitalization committee. Too many cities tear down the old and build new. Deer Creek Falls believes in saving the old. Many small rural towns have slowly died when the younger generations drift away, the community atmosphere dying along with them. The revitalization committee focuses on increasing tourism and providing a safe and welcoming place to live. I'm proud to be a member."

"What would it mean to you to win the contest?"

Alexis paused. "Being part of the contest is important because of the amazing and thoughtful contribution to our veterans. But the icing on the cake would be to remodel the Whitmore Estate. I had the chance to tour the house when Old Man Whitmore passed. The moment I stepped into the majestic home, I knew I wanted to bring it back to its former glory. Just thinking about the history of the home gives me goosebumps." Alexis rubbed her arms. "My friend Maggie had the same reaction, and we've dreamt of getting our hands on that estate ever since." She hoped she didn't sound too corny.

James asked a few more questions and then stood to put away his camera. "Thanks for taking the time to be interviewed and for granting permission to post it on the city's web page. Chloe will upload both yours and Raven's interviews soon." James snapped the camera case closed as a knock sounded on the door.

"Excuse me, James." Alexis opened the door to Susan and Elsie.

"I hope you're done with the interview. We brought a late lunch." Susan greeted her with a hug. "The American Legion had their annual Booyah Feed."

"We just finished. That's so sweet. I forgot all about it, come on in." Elsie came through the door carrying a large pot. "Let me take that for you." Her stomach growled at the aroma.

She led the way to the kitchen. Susan kissed her husband on the cheek on her way through the house.

"What a beautiful kitchen, Alexis." Susan ran her hand along the black granite countertop.

"Alexis and Maggie could create a beautiful kitchen for you too. I'm so proud of my girl . . . both my girls." Elsie side-hugged Alexis, bringing her in close. "Maggie and Alexis work well together."

"Well, she has my vote," Susan said, eyeing her husband.

"Thank you for bringing lunch, that was really nice of you both." Alexis turned the heat on under the pot and pulled bowls from the cupboard.

They sat around the table enjoying the conversation and the rich broth packed full of short ribs, chicken, and vegetables. She appreciated that Susan and Elsie didn't try to sell her talents any further in front of James. Her work spoke for itself. She was talented and could handle a large estate remodel.

She was wondering how Elsie had happened upon Susan bringing dinner over when Elsie spoke up. "Chloe has done such a wonderful job with the city website. The presentation at the meeting had all of us in tears."

"Oh. I forgot the revitalization committee met today. What had you in tears?" Concern etched Alexis's face.

"The blooper reel Chloe put together," Elsie announced.

Alexis stopped with her spoon at her lips. "Bloopers?"

Susan giggled. "Emma is such a card. When she said she peed a little, I think I did too."

James shook his head at his wife's hilarity.

"There's a blooper reel?" Alexis's face flushed.

James leaned over and stage-whispered, "It's mostly of Zeke. I would never jeopardize your reputation."

Elsie placed a reassuring hand on hers. "You'll have complete say in what is posted. What Chloe showed us was a presentation for our eyes only."

Alexis released the breath she hadn't realized she was holding. She needed to see this blooper reel, but first she needed to get ready for her date.

CHAPTER FIFTEEN

*I*n Alexis's experience, old back injuries—much like your monthly "friend" arriving complete with cramps, discomfort, and the need for medication—tended to creep up at times that just weren't convenient. Times like, for instance, the third blind date her friends had arranged for her.

Bent over at the waist, Alexis clutched her mid back. Having it seize up in the middle of the already-uncomfortable encounter was bad enough, but what worried her even more was that she had a set of cabinets to hang tomorrow and not enough guys to get the job done without her.

"Are you okay?" Date Number Three asked. How had she forgotten his name? What was she supposed to say? That she was fine? She wasn't in the mood to deal with a blind date, especially one who stood at five foot seven—three inches shorter than her. What was Lily thinking?

"Nope. Not okay. My back went out. I need to head home."

"Oh. Okay. What can I do to help?"

Cringing and taking short breaths through the pain, she limped her way through the crowd of gyrating dancers, Date Number Three following behind. Her head pounded from the strobe lights.

She felt eighty-two, not twenty-eight. Luckily, she'd worn leggings under her skirt, so her backside wasn't on display as she limped her way to the exit.

She winced as she assessed the likelihood of getting in and out of her date's sports car, the seat inches from the ground.

"Could you call Lily? Her car may be easier to get in and out of."

"Of course, right away."

～

TEN MINUTES LATER, Lily double-parked in front of the night club. "Oh my gosh, Alexis. What happened?"

"An old back injury. I just need to lie on the couch for a day and it'll right itself." Lily wrapped an arm around Alexis's side to support her as she helped her into her car. Alexis whispered through gritted teeth, "What's my date's name again?"

Lily snickered. "Josh. It went that well, huh?"

Alexis had to give the guy credit; he had stayed with her and kept her company until Lily arrived.

Josh stood by the car door while Lily helped Alexis into the seat, helped her swing her legs in, and fastened her seat belt.

"Thanks, Josh, and I'm really sorry I ruined your night."

"Don't be sorry. I heard tall girls sometimes have back problems."

"Okay then. Bye." It was too bad he couldn't see her eye roll.

"Even his feet are small," Alexis said when she was alone in the car with Lily, noticing only because she'd been bent over.

"Well, you dodged a bullet, I guess. You know what they say about small feet." Lily laughed as she pulled into traffic.

Alexis shuddered. "Well, it's a good thing my back went out."

～

WHEN THEY TURNED down Alexis's street, she could see Zeke standing in her driveway. "Lily, who called Zeke?"

"I did. I texted him and told him I'd gone to rescue you. He said he'd be at your house when I arrived, to help you get settled. I ran out on my shift at Rosie's, and I need to get back and close. I'm sorry your date didn't go well," Lily said. "I really hoped you two would hit it off."

She pulled into Alexis's driveway, and Zeke opened the passenger door.

Lily moved to help, but Zeke stopped her. "I've got her, Lily. Thanks for calling me."

"I'm sorry I have to run. Feel better, Alexis. You're in good hands, but call me if you need anything."

"Thanks for coming to my rescue, Lily. I'll text you later."

ZEKE HAD ALREADY UNLOCKED Alexis's front door with his spare key. He wasn't thrilled she'd gone on another date. She should have been on a date with him, but he'd wait until she fulfilled her commitment to her friends before swooping in.

"Another date, huh?"

"Yep." Alexis winced at the pain as she climbed her front steps.

He probably wouldn't earn any points by teasing her when she was in pain. "Maybe I should take you to the hospital."

"No, just get me to the couch and I'll be fine. It's happened before and all I need is rest. I've been pushing myself and not getting enough sleep. I also need to remember to stretch, which I have not done."

Zeke was tempted to ask where and how she'd thrown out her back, but he didn't really want to know.

He helped Alexis lower herself onto her leather sofa but

almost fell on top of her. Their faces close, Alexis gasped, and he scrambled to his feet. "Did I hurt you?"

She took a deep breath and exhaled. "No. I'm good."

He removed her boots and covered her with a throw blanket. "What can I get you?"

"Can you grab my pillow from my bed, a glass of water, and some ibuprofen?"

"Yep. Don't move. I'll be right back," he said.

He could see the worry lines on her face. Alexis was working overtime to meet the contest deadline. Without her, he felt a little panicked too. His goal was to keep her still, help her any way he could, distract her from the overwhelming amount of work they needed to accomplish on the jobsites, and still be there for her. He found the meds, filled a glass of water, and went into her room to grab her pillow. He breathed in her coconut scent, wishing she'd chosen him to date rather than the duds she'd been out with recently.

"Here you go. Let's lean you forward a bit." Zeke positioned the pillow behind Alexis's head. He handed her two ibuprofen and held the glass to her lips.

"Can I get you anything else?"

"Yeah. Help me get up." She tried to sit up, but he gently pushed her back down.

"Maybe if I stretch, the spasms will subside," she said.

"No way, you need to rest."

Zeke settled into the chair next to her and paged through the latest *Best Builder* magazine as he waited for Maggie to bring dinner. Alexis had just dozed off when he heard a knock on the front door.

Alexis moved to get up.

"Stay," Zeke said. "I'll get it. It's Maggie. I asked her grab food before she headed home."

· · ·

MAGGIE CARRIED in a takeout bag from Rosie's that smelled heavenly and made Alexis's stomach growl. She handed the bag to Zeke.

"Unfortunately, I can only stay a few minutes. But I see you're in good hands." Maggie placed the latest book club book on the coffee table. "Just in case you can join us next month. How are you doing?"

"I'm okay, but I need to use the bathroom and since you're here, I could use some help getting my pj's on."

"No problem. I'm guessing that's why Zeke called me. Can you swing your legs over and I'll help you up?"

Maggie and Zeke both stayed close as she hobbled to the bathroom.

After Maggie helped her change, Alexis decided it was best to stay in bed.

When Maggie left, Zeke came into her bedroom with a tube of pain-relieving cream. "Turn over. Massage time."

Usually when Alexis's back was sore, she'd turn the massaging jets on high and soak in the hot tub until her muscles relaxed. She didn't know if having Zeke's strong hands kneading her back would be wise. "Are you sure?"

"Alexis."

She did need to be back on her feet tomorrow, and her hot tub was out of the question. She'd had a hard enough time making it to her bedroom. "Okay."

Zeke pulled back the covers as she painfully maneuvered onto her stomach and when she was settled, he lifted her pajama top.

He knew this was a bad idea because he couldn't help but visualize all the places his hands could roam. "This is going to be cold." He squirted the ointment onto her lower back and began massaging. He tried to hold it together while she made soft sighing noises. He'd had lower back issues and knew he needed to massage her gluteus medius if she had any chance of working tomorrow.

ALEXIS TRIED NOT TO MOAN, but Zeke's hands were strong and sensual. With her eyes closed, she pictured his fingers wandering lower and moving more material aside. When he lowered her pajama pants a little, she gasped and moved her hips slightly. Her mind filled with all kinds of sexual fantasies.

"Breathe, Alexis."

Had she stopped breathing? How could he tell?

His thumbs worked their magic, and she couldn't help but moan again. If only she could see his face; was he as affected as she was?

"Zeke?"

He stopped massaging, leaving a hand resting gently on her upper back, and bent down. "Am I hurting you?"

"I wish I had been on a date with *you* tonight."

Zeke's hands left her back and righted her pajamas. "I wish I had asked you."

Alexis eased onto her side, trying to get comfortable. "Can you put a pillow between my knees?"

Zeke reached for a flat throw pillow and inched her knees apart. How could she be in two types of pain at the same time? she thought to herself. Her back and the pain of knowing Zeke's hands would be soothing in other ways.

Laying a soft kiss on her cheek, Zeke ran his hand down her side and kissed her again on the head. "I'll sleep on the couch tonight if you need anything."

"Can you sleep next to me?"

"Are you sure?"

The only thing she wasn't sure about was whether it was the pain meds making her bold, or his touch. "I'm sure."

Zeke fell asleep on top of the covers because he didn't trust himself. When he woke in the middle of the night, a blanket covered his body. He had heard Alexis get up once but didn't let on he was awake. He watched her closely as she walked into the bathroom. Definitely straighter than hours before. There was still no way she'd be limber enough to help on the jobsite.

At five a.m. the alarm on his watch buzzed. He slid out of bed and stepped out of the house to call his mom. "Hi, Mom. Did I wake you?"

"No, I'm on my second cup of coffee already. Are you calling about Alexis? How is she?"

"Not in any shape to work, but I don't know if she would agree."

"What can I do?"

"I hoped you'd come over and stay with her. Keep her from working today. I'm heading to the jobsite in a little while."

"Say no more. I'll be there in ten minutes."

"Thanks, Mom, you're the best."

ZEKE RAN HOME when his mom arrived, started the coffee, and hopped into the shower. He arrived at the contest home just as Evan, the crew chief, pulled into the driveway.

"How's Alexis?" Evan asked, stepping out of his truck.

"Walking straighter, but not one hundred percent. Give her until tomorrow and she'll be here, no matter if she's fully recovered or not."

"I can't believe she's not resisting."

"I called in reinforcements. My mom is at her house to keep her from coming in."

Evan laughed. "Good. The cabinet makers should be here any minute."

"Yep, that's why I'm here. I'm ready to help and to take orders."

A panel truck pulled to the curb just as they stepped inside and turned on the lights.

They had the cabinets installed in under five hours. Zeke and Evan stepped back and admired their work. "Looks good," Zeke said.

"That it does. The countertops are due in tomorrow. I could use some muscle if you're willing to come back."

"I'll be here, and I'll bring the boss. Her favorite time in the remodel is when the cabinets go in."

"I'm sure it's killing her not to be here."

"Yeah, I thought for sure she would have stopped by. My mom's a miracle worker." Zeke glanced at his watch. "Don't you have kids to pick up from school?"

"I do. I better get going. I'd be back, but there's not much to do until tomorrow."

"I'll lock up. Go ahead."

"Thanks. I don't want to be late again."

Evan was a single dad of three girls and most of the time, the neighbor lady picked them up from school and watched them until he got home, but she was in Florida visiting her daughter.

Evan's situation was similar to Zeke's brother Roman's: his wife had walked away from her family and her marriage. "Say hi to the girls," Zeke said.

"Will do. Thanks, Zeke."

The sun hadn't set yet, but the day was cold and dreary with a high in the mid 40s. When he stepped out of the house, a soft mewing caught his attention. He stood still and listened, then walked down the stairs opposite the ramp and peeked under the shrubs. "Hey, little one. What are you doing under there?" A small black kitten with large yellow eyes watched him with apprehension. "Come on, buddy. I won't hurt you." He held out his hand, hoping the kitten was curious enough to step within his reach so he could pull him out of his hiding spot. It was going to be too cold and wet tonight for the little guy to be out here with little shelter.

The kitten inched forward, and Zeke wrapped his hand around him, pulling him to rest in his arms. "There you are." The kitten shivered and Zeke tucked him inside his jacket. "Who do you belong to?" The neighbor pulled into her drive, and he walked over.

"Say, does this little guy belong to you?" Zeke asked as she stepped out of her car. He'd seen the middle-aged woman with salt-and-pepper hair around town but didn't know her name.

She shook her head. "I've never seen him before, but we've had both cats and dogs dropped off in the past. I watched a car pull up and open their door one day last winter, and out jumped a dog. They drove away before I could get their license plate. She's mine now, but I can't take them all in. Best dog I've ever owned." The woman shook her head again. "Sometimes I prefer animals over people."

"I hear you there. Thanks. I'm going to take this one home, but if you hear of anyone looking for him, let me know. I'm working on the house next door."

"I recognize you. You're Linnie Reynolds's son, right? I've been on the contest website. That's a nice thing the Hennings are doing. Your blooper reels are hilarious. My vote is for Alexis."

"Yep, Linnie's my mom. I'm Zeke. Thanks for your vote."

"Well, I better get in. Sadie will need to be let out."

Zeke turned the seat warmer and heat on high in his truck and made a makeshift bed out of his jacket on the front seat. The kitten curled up and fell asleep before he pulled away from the curb.

ZEKE STEPPED through Alexis's back door with the kitten in his arms. "Honey, I'm home!"

He heard Alexis chuckle. He set two grocery bags on the island and walked into the living room, where Alexis lay on the floor with her legs resting on the couch cushion, her eyes focused on the ceiling.

He leaned over her and looked down. "Does that help?"

"Very much. It takes the pressure off my lower back."

"How are you feeling?"

"Much better. I've been walking around in the upright position."

Zeke chuckled. "Good. I brought you something."

"You did?"

"Uh-huh." He kneeled on the floor and placed the kitten on her chest.

She squealed in delight.

"He's yours if you want him, but—"

"Yes!"

"Yes, you want him?" Zeke grinned.

"Yes. I want him. Are you sure it's a boy?"

"Yep. I looked."

The kitten curled up on Alexis's chest, purred, and stretched.

"Where did you get him?"

"Found him under the bushes at the Elmhurst house."

"Really? Did you check if he belonged to anyone nearby?"

Zeke flipped around, lay back, and placed his feet on the couch, mirroring Alexis. "I did. Talked to the neighbor, who thought maybe he'd been dropped off."

"What!? Oh, poor guy." Alexis stroked his fur, a smile on her face. Zeke sure loved her smile.

"Does he have a name?" she asked.

"Nope. I thought you'd like to name him."

"Boo."

"Boo?"

"Yep, Boo. Look at him—he's so cute! All black with not a stitch of white anywhere." The kitten stretched, and she lifted him up to inspect him. "Nope, no white."

Zeke enjoyed making Alexis happy.

CHAPTER SIXTEEN

*A*lexis had behaved like a true contractor this week, delegating the work instead of getting involved. She needed to save her back from any unnecessary stress. Her crew stayed on track, even with her not engaging in any heavy lifting or pitching in, a true measure of the competency and hard work of her team. She didn't even mind James filming as she talked with her crew and checked in on their progress.

After visiting with Pete and checking on the church renovation, Alexis sent a quick text to Zeke: *I'm heading home. Can we do popcorn night tonight?*

She didn't have to wait long for his response: *Yes. Text me if we need anything and I'll stop by the grocery store.* A kiss emoji followed.

Not knowing how to react, she didn't. She stopped at home and visited Boo, filled his food dish, and played with him before heading to Zeke's house. She stood in Zeke's kitchen, working the crank on the old-fashioned stovetop popcorn maker. About once a month, she and Zeke got together to catch up on their favorite show, *Counting Cars*, with two heaping bowls of popcorn with white cheddar powder sprinkled generously on top. Between the two renovations, working six days a week, and Zeke's trip to LA, they had a backlog of four episodes to watch.

Zeke came in and set a grocery bag on the island. He pulled out two boxes of Junior Mints and placed them next to the popcorn tubs. "Mmmm, smells good."

Alexis dumped the popcorn into two large bowls, dividing the contents equally. She set the kettle back on the stove and continued stirring the last few kernels.

Zeke washed his hands at the sink. He turned off the stove, moved the pot off the burner, and turned her around to face him. "How are you feeling?"

"Good as new."

"So, we're only catching up on the show?"

Alexis moved in closer. "Well, maybe not only the show."

"Too bad your hot water heater was replaced."

"Oh yeah, why's that?"

"I like when you use my shower." Zeke stepped closer and placed a tentative kiss on her lips, then wrapped his muscular arms around her. Being in his arms felt like home. She felt brave and skimmed her lips along his neck, planting gentle kisses. When he backed her into the island, the heat in his gaze threatened to melt her on the spot. She wondered if he could read all the inappropriate thoughts running through her head. Their lips came together, tentative at first, and when she whimpered, he deepened the kiss. She didn't know how she'd ever resisted kissing him before now. How could one kiss be so full of passion?

Zeke's phone blasted with an incoming call. She recognized the *Mission: Impossible* ringtone. Luke. The moment ruined. Zeke rested his forehead against hers. "I should get that." The deep timbre of his voice told her he wasn't happy about the intrusion.

Breathless and reeling from the toe-curling kiss, she smoothed down her shirt and said, "Yep. Luke may have work for you."

He picked up his phone and answered. "Hey. What's up?" He reached for her hand to keep her from walking away. "Thanks, that sounds great. Yep. Let me know. Will do." He hung up.

"Do you have to go?" Alexis asked. She hoped not. She'd been looking forward to a relaxing night with Zeke ever since he'd worked his magic on her back.

"Nope. Luke wanted to give me an update on a former case."

"He didn't have a job for you?"

Zeke lifted her chin to make her look at him. "No new job."

He traced a finger along her jaw. "I need a shower. Want to join me?" he asked, his voice husky.

Boy, did she ever. She sucked in her bottom lip. "So tempting. But we need to take whatever this is, slow. I've got too much riding on these jobs right now, and you're a distraction." His eyes held disappointment, so she hurried on. "An ohh-so-tempting distraction."

Zeke placed a quick kiss on her lips. "I won't be long." He winked. "I'll leave the door open in case you change your mind."

Omigod, she wanted to change her mind. She couldn't keep her heart from racing and the butterflies from taking flight when he was around, but she reeled in her feelings and filled two glasses with ice water.

She heard the shower shut off and minutes later, Zeke joined her on the oversized leather sofa. Their thighs touched as he sank into the cushion. She breathed in the scent of his musky body wash and wished she had accepted his invitation. His hair, still slightly damp, curled at the nape of his neck.

He picked up the remote and scrolled through the episodes.

Alexis crossed her wool-socked feet at the ankles on top of the sofa table. Zeke resumed his normal position, mimicking hers. He hadn't said anything. Just sat down like they were back to being friends. Technically they were friends, but the brief make-out session in the kitchen earlier and the invitation to join him in the shower had her wondering how to classify their new connection. Should she ask? Man, she hated this part of a budding relationship.

Alexis watched Zeke watch *Counting Cars*. She couldn't concentrate on the show when all she could think about was the kiss and the invitation she turned down moments ago.

"If you keep staring at me, I'm going to have a hard time controlling myself." He still held the remote but didn't look at her.

She giggled, and he wrapped an arm around her and drew her close. She rested her head on his shoulder.

While they watched back-to-back episodes they fell into the comfortable silence of friendship. It didn't stop her from stealing glances at him. His brow furrowed when he concentrated and after stuffing his mouth full of popcorn, he licked his lips. She hadn't made a dent in her bowl and hadn't a clue what was happening on the show. Watching Zeke made her tingle in all the right places.

He reached into her popcorn bowl and grabbed a handful, asking out of the blue, "Would you ever get back together with Ryan?"

Alexis pulled her feet off the table and placed one leg under the other. "Ah. No. Rest assured, that would never happen." She shifted on the couch so she could face him.

"What brought this up?" she asked.

Zeke shifted his body, too, turning toward her. "He stopped by the house looking for you today."

"Did you ask him what he wanted?"

"I did, and he said he'd catch you later."

"Did I ever tell you why we broke up?"

"Nope." Zeke popped a few kernels into his mouth, trying to act like what she was about to say wouldn't be a big deal. He picked up the remote and paused the show.

"I caught Ryan and Raven together at one of the houses we all worked on. I was supposed to be on another jobsite but had forgotten something. When I walked in, they were coming out of a closet, adjusting their clothing. Ryan had that deer-in-the-headlights look while he stuffed his shirt back into his pants, and Raven just looked smug."

Zeke would love to deck the guy, but he didn't want it to end up as gossip on the Town Talk app—or worse, jeopardize the contest. He sat forward and placed a hand on Alexis's thigh. "I'm sorry. I'd never cheat on you. He's an idiot. What did you do?"

"I was mad as hell but held it together. Well . . . sort of." Alexis grinned her up-to-no-good grin. "I grabbed the closest thing I could find and sawed it in half."

Zeke cringed but laughed. "Do tell."

"Ryan had an expensive piece of decorative trim sitting by the miter saw . . . I'm guessing he had just finished cutting it to size before he *finished* Raven." She grimaced. "I cut it into pieces and walked out the door."

"How expensive?"

"Priceless, to him. He had rescued it from a house . . . he couldn't wait to see it in place." Alexis smirked and sat back, grabbed the bowl back from Zeke, and pushed play on the remote.

Man, he loved Alexis. His protective nature kicked into high gear. He wrapped her in his arms and never wanted to let go. No way would that little *shit* get near her again.

The show ended with a daughter seeing her father's 1967 Mustang GT Fastback restored. The woman cried when the mechanic pulled the car out of the garage. Alexis fought back tears.

Zeke pulled her in close and kissed her temple. "Are you crying?"

"No." She wiped her eyes, then buried her head into his shoulder.

"Are too." He chuckled and started tickling her, and she sat up and tickled him back. Screw it. He couldn't resist her any longer. Sitting beside Alexis for the past few hours had about killed him. With little effort, Zeke positioned her onto his lap, and she straddled him willingly.

Their faces inches apart, Alexis stared at his lips and said, "Hi." He thought he might lose it right there and then.

He took her face in his hands and kissed her mouth—soft, sweet, and salty.

WAKING TO SOFT SNORES, Alexis bolted out of bed. She landed hard on the hardwood floor. Wait. She wasn't in bed; she had slept on the couch . . . with Zeke. Last night's escapades were slowly creeping into her memory. From where she sat on the floor, she could see Zeke's bare chest and two buttons undone on his jeans. She bit her lip at the sight of the dark hair below his navel disappearing into his pants. She looked herself over, smoothed her T-shirt down, and spied her discarded bra wrapped around the table leg.

"Good morning," Zeke said, the corners of his mouth tilted slightly upward.

She scanned his face. A smile graced his kissable lips. They'd made out like teenagers last night but didn't go further than third base. Not that she didn't want to, but she couldn't. Not now, when her career was on the line. She needed to focus on winning the contest.

"Good   morning." She had to clear her throat. Be it sleepiness or pure, unadulterated want with a touch of *take me now*, she wasn't sure. "I'll start the coffee." She stood and untangled her slate-blue satin bra being held captive by the table, and sprinted toward the bathroom. First things first. Another great reason for

short hair, she thought as she stared at herself in the mirror, bed—
or rather couch—mussed hair looked sexy instead of like a rat's
nest. She finger-combed her hair, brushed her teeth with an
unopened toothbrush she found, and headed for the kitchen.

She busied herself with grinding the coffee beans. Zeke came
up behind her and kissed her neck. A slight moan escaped at his
touch, and she tilted her neck to give him better access. What was
she doing? She needed to put a stop to this behavior, but her brain
wasn't connecting with her hips as she ground into his morning
erection.

He reached around her and ran his hands over her bra,
cupping her breasts. He whispered in her ear, "I thought we
discarded this last night."

"Mmm. Yeah." Her brain wasn't functioning.

Alexis's phone rang, pulling her out of the moment. She
sighed, breathless, and glanced at the digital readout on the
microwave: seven a.m. Zeke looked to the ceiling, trying no
doubt to contain his thoughts.

She picked up her phone. "It's Susan," she said to Zeke, and
answered. "Good morning, Susan."

CHAPTER SEVENTEEN

*A*lexis met Zeke on the sidewalk in front of her house. The afternoon was cool and the sky clear. Leaf-peeping season was in full bloom, and the leaves, in scarlet, caramelized bronze, honey gold, and eggplant, rustled slightly in the breeze. "Hey, Sweets," Zeke greeted her, wrapping her in a hug and placing a quick kiss on her lips. They'd decided to walk into town together, since she was on her way to meet Paige and Maggie at the crochet club at Turner Books, and Zeke was meeting Ethan and Owen for dinner at the Deer Creek Lodge's restaurant, the Blue Ox.

"When did you learn to crochet?" Zeke said.

"Ha! I don't know how, but I guess I'm going to learn. I've been told I need a hobby."

Zeke chuckled. "Maggie's advice?"

"How'd you know?" She didn't know if she would like to crochet or not, but she wanted to spend time with her friends. If she learned a new skill, so be it. If she didn't like it, she'd still attend when she could and enjoy their company as they worked on their projects.

It had been Lily's idea to start the crochet club after Paige took over Turner Books and remodeled, designating the back third as a gathering space for book clubs and art classes led by local artisans.

A quick and brassy horn sounded behind them. "Hello, you two!" The Sampson brothers, dressed in their Sunday best, waved as they sped past, driving their souped-up golf cart toward home.

Alexis and Zeke turned the corner onto Main Street just as the Sampsons' golf cart careened into the back of Nick's patrol car and onto the sidewalk.

"Call 911," Zeke said before sprinting toward the octogenarians. Alexis got on the phone with dispatch. Nick ran out of the café, almost hitting her with the door. He spoke into his shoulder mic as he ran down the sidewalk.

"I called the paramedics," Alexis said as she kept pace with Nick.

Zeke, a first responder, had reached the brothers first. The golf cart sat hung up on the curb at an angle. The cart had sustained the most damage. The squad car's taillight had shattered, and a purple streak from the customized golf cart ran the length of the back bumper.

When Nick and Alexis approached, Zeke had a grin on his face as one brother yelled at the other.

"Why did you push the accelerator, Eddie!?" Charlie yelled.

"I was distracted."

Alexis bent over and placed a hand on Charlie's shoulder. Dr. Sampson had once comforted her after an accident when she was fourteen. "Are you hurting anywhere, Doc?"

"No, hon. I'm fine. As for Eddie . . . I'll be doing the driving from now on." He focused his anger and embarrassment on his brother.

Charlie waved his hands around. "What would you do with a hooker, Eddie? You can barely tie your shoes!"

Concerned, Alexis looked to Nick and Zeke for answers,

trying to make sense of the brothers' ramblings. They'd seemed fine seconds ago, but now both of them were talking nonsense about hookers. Maybe they'd knocked their heads together during the crash.

Paige ran out of the bookstore. "Oh my! What happened? Is everyone okay? Doc? Eddie? Are you all right?" she asked.

"We're fine," Charlie said. "Just a little bump on the head. It doesn't even hurt." He pointed a shaky, spotted hand at the sign in front of Turner Books. "Eddie was distracted. When did you start running a bordello out of the bookstore, Miss Turner?"

"Umm, Paige . . ." Nick and Zeke's shoulders shook as they pointed to the sign.

Paige covered her mouth in shock.

Zeke smirked. "When did you start advertising for hookers?"

The chalkboard sidewalk sign read *Hookers Wanted: All Ages Welcome. Use back entrance.*

Paige stuttered, "I . . . oh."

Alexis pressed her lips together tightly to keep from laughing.

Lily came running through the small crowd that had gathered around the Sampson brothers. "It's my fault!" she wailed. "I made the sign to get attention for our crochet club."

The paramedics arrived and placed a bandage on Eddie's arm where he'd scraped it driving into the squad car.

Nick raised a brow and managed to say with a straight face, "Lily, it worked, but it probably wasn't a good idea to put a sign like that on a busy thoroughfare."

Lily turned three shades of red. "I'll erase it."

"I'll pay for the damage to your car," Paige said to Nick.

"Don't worry, Del will buff it out for me."

Alexis brought her vehicle to Del for servicing too—heck, everyone did, since Del was the only mechanic in town.

Satisfied that the Sampson brothers weren't badly hurt, Alexis joined Paige and Lily. Paige bumped Lily's shoulder and whispered, "Really clever, Lily. Too bad more people didn't see it."

Lily erased *Hookers Wanted* and replaced it with *Crochet group, use back entrance.*

"Ladies, have fun. Text us when you wrap up for the night," Zeke said and took off toward the lodge.

Nick escorted the brothers into the squad car, promising them he'd arrange to have the golf cart inspected for safety. The front axle would need some work.

Alexis waved to the brothers.

She and Lily followed Paige into Turner Books, and Paige locked the door behind them.

"Something smells good," Alexis said, and Lily agreed.

The back room had small cushioned chairs and end tables scattered around the generous space, and a larger meeting table, used for everything from art classes to community meetings, had been pushed to the side and now held a crock pot of soup and a selection of desserts. Alexis's stomach grumbled.

A steady stream of women of all ages, carrying food and tote bags full of yarn, entered the room. Alexis greeted Zeke's family with hugs. Maggie, Elsie, Emma, and Linnie talked a mile a minute as they plated cookies and bars and ladled Linnie's white chicken chili into bowls.

A knock on the doorframe had them all turning to look at the newcomer.

"Hi. Um, is this where the crochet club is meeting?"

Maggie set her plate down and walked toward the timid teenager. "Yes. Hi, Sloane. Welcome! Please, come in. I'm so glad you're joining us." She wrapped her in a hug.

Alexis joined them. "Hi, Sloane. It's nice to see you."

Sloane smiled. "You too." She looked around at the group of ladies. "I brought a snack. I wasn't sure if I should, but my dad encouraged me to. I think he wanted me to make my Cashew Crunch so he could have some."

Maggie took the container, sneaked a small handful of the cashew-and-Fritos mixture, and placed it on the table next to a small fridge and a tray of cookies. "Snacks are not required but are definitely appreciated, even though your dad benefited. The fridge is full of water, both plain and flavored, or if you prefer coffee, I can make a pot. Help yourself and sit anywhere."

Sloane chose the chair next to Alexis and Maggie. Which made sense since their frequent visits to her father's hardware store probably made them the most familiar faces in the room.

Alexis asked Sloane, "Do you know how to crochet? So far, I think I'm the only one here who doesn't."

"I do. My dad taught me when I was little."

Lily, pulling a bright turquoise yarn from her bag, said, "Really? Nate knows how to crochet?"

Alexis watched in amazement as Lily addressed Sloane without looking at the project she worked on.

"He still remembers from taking a class in high school." Sloane pulled a few stuffed orange and brown pieces from her bag.

"Good for him," Emma said.

Maggie nodded. "We all learned in our Home Economics class." Maggie hitched a thumb at Paige. "Paige wasn't very good; her nose was always in books."

"Hey!" Paige pretended to be offended. "She's right. I have no idea what I'm doing." She held up what looked like a scarf, or maybe the start of a sweater, to prove her point.

"I was your dad's art teacher. If I remember right, he was quite talented." Emma pulled a chevron-patterned blanket in soft pastels from her bag.

Not sure where to start, Alexis held a pair of needles like chopsticks. "What are you working on, Sloane?"

"I like making animals. This one will be a giraffe." She held up a pattern book with a cute stuffed giraffe and cat on the cover. "I gave the cat to sheriff Nick," she explained. "Nick keeps stuffed animals in the back of his car in case a child needs comforting."

"That's so sweet," Alexis said.

The others nodded and voiced their agreement.

Ruth Reid, mother of Chloe and Nick, walked in. "Sorry I'm late." She took a bottle of water from the fridge and sat next to Emma. "So, Lily, I heard you caused quite the ruckus out front."

Lily covered her face with her hands. "My crochet club back east referred to themselves as the Happy Hookers. I thought the sign would turn heads and we'd get more people to sign up. I didn't think it would cause an accident." She held her hand over her heart. "To think I was responsible for two sweet old men getting hurt."

"You did nothing wrong, Lily." Alexis said.

"They shouldn't have been driving so fast and should have looked where they were going," Emma scoffed.

"Thank goodness they weren't seriously hurt," Maggie said.

Maggie handed Alexis a small ball of light gray yarn and held up her single hook. "You don't eat with them, plus you only need one—we're crocheting, not knitting."

Alexis grinned.

"Let's start you off practicing a slip knot and a chain." Maggie showed her how to make the knot and after a few tries, she was successful. Although frustrating at first, she got the hang of chaining, too, but thought she'd stick to reading as her hobby.

Paige looked up from her project and asked Rachel, "Where is Levi tonight?"

"I dropped him off at Roman's. The twins are looking after him."

"How's everything going between you and Nick?" Emma asked with one brow raised.

Always the matchmaker. But Alexis knew from what Zeke had said about Nick and Rachel that they were only friends. They'd both lost someone they loved: Rachel, her husband; and Nick, his best friend. He had promised his buddy he'd look after his wife and little boy if anything happened to him.

"I already had the love of my life. I don't know if I'll ever be ready to date again. Nick's a great guy, and Levi adores him." Rachel swallowed hard. "He's been a wonderful friend. Nothing more."

Emma patted her knee, and Lily and Chloe side-hugged her.

"I'm glad Nick talked you into moving to our small town," Ruth said. "We are happy you joined our crazy little community."

"Thanks, Ruth."

"I heard Zeke stayed at Mandy Blake's home in California," Lily said.

The last thing Alexis wanted to talk about was Zeke's involvement with the sexy actress, so she kept her head down, concentrating on the next chain stitch.

Maggie spoke up. "There's nothing going on between Zeke and Mandy Blake. He was there to do a job."

Sloane leaned toward Alexis. "You're doing great."

When Alexis looked up to acknowledge Sloane, everyone's eyes were on her. "What?"

"Oh. Nothing, dear." Emma and Elsie grinned at her.

Her face flushed. How could they possibly know she and Zeke had transitioned into new territory?

Several hours later, with a full stomach and a very long chain, she packed away her project, as did the rest of the crocheters. She hadn't escaped all talk of Zeke, but she did manage to steer the conversation away from anything personal. She learned a lot about the recent goings-on in town since she hadn't had time to check the Town Talk app, and viewed several bloopers of Zeke at the house on Maggie's phone.

Alexis sent a quick text to Zeke: *I think they all know. Done here.*

She and Maggie stayed behind to help Paige clean up.

Paige glanced at her phone. "Our guys are out front, waiting."

Alexis liked the idea of Zeke being her guy. That was, until they reached the sidewalk. The three of them stopped in their tracks as they watched a woman jump into Zeke's arms and wrap her legs around his waist.

What was Mandy Blake doing here in Deer Creek Falls?

CHAPTER EIGHTEEN

*C*hicken: the word used for the cowardly avoidance of something or, in Alexis's case, some*one*. Alexis had visions of running into Maggie Blake leaving Zeke's place all flushed and tousled, and she didn't think she could handle that, so she hurried out of bed, showered, dressed, and arrived at the church before five a.m. When she unlocked the door and flipped on the lights, her phone alerted her of an incoming text. She groaned. Zeke.

Are you avoiding me?

She sucked in her lower lip. She didn't want to lie, but she didn't want to talk about her sudden departure last night. She pictured Mandy Blake's legs wrapped around him and placed a finger to her temple, fighting off a headache. Maggie had called last night to assure her Mandy Blake only stopped to see the town Zeke had made sound "irresistible and quaint" and to see for herself that Zeke was all right after being injured saving her life.

Alexis didn't believe that for a minute. Duluth's airport was an hour away, and it didn't have any direct flights to New York or Los Angeles.

She texted Zeke back: *Tommy called last night, his mom is*

sick, he needed to stay home today. I'll be working at the church all day.

Her phone rang and she answered on an exasperated breath. "Hey, Zeke."

"There's nothing going on with me and Mandy Blake. She headed back to Duluth last night."

"Okay. Say, can you set the light fixtures today and make sure the plumber stays on task? I really need you to get things squared away at the Elmhurst house."

"As long as you're not avoiding me."

"Zeke, I need to go. I have a long day at the church, and I'm heading to Maggie's tonight to carve pumpkins."

"Maybe I'll see you there."

"Sure. We can talk later."

Avoiding Zeke, or staying annoyed with him, wasn't easy. He texted throughout the day with funny emojis that made her laugh. Pete shook his head each time he caught her looking at her phone. When they finished installing the kitchen appliances, they contemplated calling it a day. Sean was working on the trim in the bedroom and bathroom.

"So, you and Zeke finally took the plunge?" Pete whispered.

Alexis glared at him. "Don't be crude, Pete."

"I think your mind is in the gutter, General, not mine."

She grumbled, "We're taking things slow."

"Your smile hasn't gone unnoticed."

Sean walked in, and Alexis gave Pete the stink eye. Pete understood and dropped the subject.

"Let's call it a night," Alexis said as she packed up her tools. "I've got pumpkins to carve. We made great progress today. Zeke will be over in the next couple days to finish the lighting and any last-minute electrical."

Sean stretched and said, "I've got a few pumpkins to carve tonight too. I'll see you guys later."

As Pete walked her out, Alexis said, "If you don't have plans tonight, a bunch of us will be at Maggie's, carving pumpkins."

"I might have a date."

"Really? Anyone I know?"

"Don't you know everyone in town?"

She smiled. "Probably. Are you going to tell me?"

"I don't want to jinx it."

Pete climbed into his truck and Alexis did the same. She didn't want to pry into his social life, so she let it go. He honked as he pulled out, and she waved. He'd piqued her curiosity. Maybe Maggie and Owen knew.

ALEXIS HADN'T CARVED a pumpkin since she was a teenager, and she wondered why she didn't buy one every Halloween. She arrived at Maggie's with her big, fat, round pumpkin, her favorite shape to carve, looking forward to the evening with Maggie and her nieces. Owen answered her knock. "Hey, Alexis. Let me take that from you."

She handed Owen her pumpkin. "Thanks." She knelt to pet Athena, Owen's Belgian Malinois. "How's my good girl?" Athena awarded her with kisses. Alexis stepped into the kitchen to a display of various-sized pumpkins set on the large granite island, and two excited girls who had already eaten their share of candy.

Nikki and Nora jumped up and down. "Hi, Alexis! Aren't these pumpkins dope?"

The sugar-induced energy radiating from the twins was intoxicating, and she giggled along with them. "They are pretty awesome. I can't wait to have my fingers oozing with pumpkin guts."

Nora grimaced. "Good. You can gut my pumpkin. That's cringy."

Maggie glanced Alexis's way when Nora used the slang term for gross. Alexis smiled at her friend. When they were young, they'd latched onto slang and used as many words as possible. They'd even made up words with hopes they'd catch on with their friends. Last week when Sloane had used the word "dope," Alexis had texted Maggie to find out what it meant. It definitely didn't have the same meaning it did in their day.

Each pumpkin sat on sheets of newspaper along with a carving knife and marker. Maggie went over the safety protocols while Alexis mimed mock rebellion, fighting pumpkins with a butter knife in hand. The girls laughed at her actions.

Owen stood and quieted everyone down. "I'd like to make this a contest."

A collaborative groan filled the kitchen, and Alexis exaggerated her eye roll for Owen's benefit.

"You too, Alexis. Whoever comes up with the most creative pumpkin wins."

She didn't want to take part in another contest, no matter how mundane a pumpkin carving contest might be.

"That's not fair, Uncle Owen," Nora said.

"Yeah, we all know who will win," Nikki countered with her hands on her hips, staring Owen down.

Alexis loved these girls and joined in on their razzing. "Yeah, *Uncle* Owen!"

Owen held up his hands in defeat. "Okay . . . not a contest. But there are prizes for everyone."

Nora cheered and Nikki asked, "What kind of prizes are we talking about?"

"That's a surprise. Now let's get to work." Owen pulled four colorful cans from a kitchen drawer and hid them behind his back. "I almost forgot. This is for after we are done carving."

Owen placed a can each next to Alexis, Nikki, Nora, and Maggie.

"Yay—silly string!" The girls jumped up and down.

Maggie smiled and announced, "Get Ready. Get Set. Go!"

When they picked up their markers, the laughing subsided and everyone became serious, concentrating on creating a prizewinning pumpkin.

Maggie bumped Alexis's shoulder and whispered, "Do you know when you concentrate, the tip of your tongue comes out."

Alexis stopped. "Yes. I'm highly aware of it, since you remind me every time it happens. Hey, do you know who Pete's seeing? He mentioned he might have a date tonight."

"No! He hasn't said anything to me." Maggie placed a finger to her lips in concentration. "He stops at the Eagle's Nest for dinner if he's not eating with us. I wonder if it's the new girl, Hannah. Maybe some recon is in order."

Alexis laughed. "Maybe."

When the girls finished, they wiped down the counters. Owen had separated the pumpkin seeds from the guts and already had three cookie sheets filled and ready to bake. Alexis loved salted pumpkin seeds and couldn't wait to snack.

They carried their silly string and jack-o-lanterns outside. They set them on the deck, and Owen placed a candle in each of them. "Maggie, why don't you do the honors and light the candles." He handed her the long grill lighter.

Everyone stepped into the yard to admire the row of orange masterpieces. Alexis pointed to Nikki's carving of a ghost flying over a cityscape, and Nora's cute owl. "Okay, I've been duped. You two are so creative." The girls beamed at the compliment. They hadn't even used templates. "Wow."

Maggie wrapped her arms around her nieces. "I think you need to help me in the shop, and I'll teach you girls to weld."

"Can we?" the girls asked in unison.

"Of course, but we'll have to ask your dad first."

The twins groaned and everyone laughed. Owen took his phone out and snapped pictures of the girls next to their pumpkins.

Alexis and Maggie stood next to each other, posing for a picture, when a hand tapped them on the shoulder. They both jumped, because seriously . . . no one was behind them when they came out to stand on the deck. They turned and screamed as they came face to face with a man in a creepy clown mask, trying to figure out which Reynolds brother it was. Alexis's eyes moved to his torso, and she knew. Zeke had scared the hell out of her.

The girls were screaming and shooting the clown with silly string. Nikki karate-chopped Zeke in the shin, and he went down and pretended he was hurt. They continued to spray him.

He pulled off his mask and yelled, "Okay, I give! I give!"

The house lights were bright enough to illuminate Zeke's form on the ground, laughing as the girls piled on top of him.

Maggie looked to her smiling husband. "Oh my gosh, you two planned this."

Owen shrugged. "Guilty."

"Hey! What's going on out here?" Roman's booming voice rang out.

That made everyone jump. They were all in hysterics, including Roman, the guilty interloper.

Maggie glared at her brothers. "It's a good thing Mom and Gram aren't here. You'd be in so much trouble."

Roman and Zeke smirked as Maggie chastised them. "Oh, come on. That was fun," Roman said.

"Who wants hot chocolate?" Maggie asked.

The girls answered at the same time, "Me!"

Owen held up four envelopes and handed them out to Maggie, Alexis, Nikki, and Nora. Nikki and Nora opened theirs and shrieked with happiness. "Fifty dollars to Rural Chic?"

Both girls ran to Owen and hugged the big softy. Maggie sighed. "He's going to make a great dad someday."

Alexis agreed. "Thanks, Owen, but you didn't need to do this."

He waved her off. "You and Maggie have been working hard. Take time out of your day and enjoy shopping."

Alexis blew him a kiss. "Thank you."

"You're welcome."

Zeke sat at the island next to her. He handed her the bowl of miniature marshmallows.

"Thanks." She plopped a handful of the sweet morsels into her steaming mug of chocolate.

Since she ran away last night, they hadn't talked. Zeke's woodsy smell engulfed her; their thighs rested comfortably together. She swallowed down the thoughts of his lips on hers and picked up the mug and sipped.

"Don't you think, Alexis?" Owen asked her.

"I'm sorry, what?"

Zeke chuckled and squeezed her thigh, then brought both hands to the counter to pick up his mug.

"I commented on how the house contest has the potential to bring new people to our area, even if they're only tourists."

"Absolutely. With the bloopers reel on social media and the hits they're generating, I can see people flocking to our town."

Roman leaned against the counter. "Yeah, who wouldn't want to see more of my brother acting like an idiot."

"Thanks. I love you too," Zeke said and popped a few pumpkin seeds into his mouth.

"It's been fun, but I have an early morning." Alexis stood and hugged Nikki and Nora. "I hope you plan to stop by my house tomorrow night."

"Yes!" both girls said. "Right, Dad?"

"I thought you were too old to trick-or-treat," Roman teased his girls.

"We aren't if we visit our family and friends," Nikki said.

Roman's smile widened as he teased his girls. He had the same dimple as Zeke, Alexis noticed.

"Okay then, I'll see you tomorrow," she said. "Owen, Maggie, thank you for a fun-filled evening. Carving a pumpkin was a great stress reliever."

"Hey, Alexis. Can I hitch a ride with you?" Zeke said.

"Where's your truck?"

"Roman gave me a ride. He had an errand he had to run in town and picked me up."

She eyed Roman. His poker face remained intact. "Sure."

Alexis knew she was being set up. She walked out the door with Zeke after twenty more minutes of saying goodbye. She wondered if people from every state in the nation congregated at the door, saying goodbyes for as long as Minnesotans seemed to. Part of her wanted to spend time with Zeke, but the thought of being stuck with him alone made her jittery.

"I can drive if you want. I haven't had any alcohol," Zeke said.

"Neither have I. My truck, I'll drive. Get in before I leave you behind."

ALEXIS WASN'T MAKING it easy for Zeke to apologize for what she'd witnessed the other night. He hadn't seen her until after Mandy's legs dropped from around his waist. Alexis had retreated into the night, but he couldn't ignore Mandy. She'd arrived in his small town, and he needed to find out why. Maggie had approached him after Mandy busied herself signing autographs, chastising him for his display with the famous actress in front of her best friend. He knew it looked bad.

When he'd arrived home, her house was dark. He was a little miffed she didn't stick around so he could introduce her to Miss Blake. He couldn't blame Alexis, especially after Maggie reminded him of his flirtatious ways Alexis had endured for years. But she doubted his intentions, and that's what hurt the most.

Alexis broke the silence. "So . . . talk. You obviously orchestrated this." She waved her hand in front of her.

"Apparently, you jumped to conclusions about Miss Blake."

"*Really*?"

The glow of the dashboard highlighted her face. He wanted to reach for her. To touch her. But he sat on his hands because Alexis didn't look happy. "Why didn't you stay so I could introduce you?"

"Oh, I don't know, Zeke . . . maybe because she had her legs wrapped around you?"

The lights from the streetlamps on Main Street lit the cab of the truck. He turned slightly and heaved in a breath. "Not my fault. She was excited to see me."

Alexis pulled into her driveway as a scattering of snowflakes fell and melted on the windshield. She hit the garage door opener and pulled in. "Was there something going on between the two of you in California?"

"No." They both exited the vehicle, and he followed her to her door. "Can I come in?"

She stopped before opening the utility door. "I'm not mad at you, Zeke. A famous actress dry-humping you in the middle of Main Street surprised me, and I realized I didn't have a claim on you, and never will."

He reached for her hand and pulled her close. She looked away and he tipped her chin to meet her gaze. Misty-eyed, she stared at him.

"That's where you're wrong," he said. "I've been *waiting* for you to claim me. I put up with the dates, and now I want you all to myself."

"I want that too."

Their mouths came together in a cascade of emotions. He hit the button to lower the garage door, scooped her legs out from under her, and carried her inside.

CHAPTER NINETEEN

*A*lexis reached out to stop the shrilling alarm. Zeke rolled over and pulled her close after she shut off the offending noise.

"Good morning," Zeke said, his voice husky with sleep.

Last night he'd exceeded all her expectations. Making love to Zeke stole her breath away, more than once. Three times . . . if she was counting. Aroused by his strong arms wrapped around her, Alexis scooted closer, nuzzling his neck. Her tongue skimmed his jawline and traced his ear. He shivered as she licked and nibbled.

"Good morning," she whispered. She straightened, straddled him, and pulled her T-shirt over her head. She hadn't been with anyone for longer than she cared to admit, and couldn't help herself. She needed him again. Now.

Fully sated, she smiled. Morning sex she could get used to, with this hotter-than-holy-hell specimen who'd *claimed* her last night . . , repeatedly.

Zeke kissed her slowly and then gathered his clothes. "I'll start the coffee on my way out."

She sat up after snuggling her pillow close. "Thanks. I'll meet you at the Elmhurst house."

"Sounds good." He bent down to kiss her, and she tried to tug him back into bed. "As much as I'd love to go another round with you, we have plumbers at the house today."

She glanced at the clock and fell back onto her pillow. "What time should I be ready for the party tonight?"

He sat on the edge of the bed. "The girls will be over to trick or treat at dusk, and then we'll leave."

"Did you buy them some candy?"

"I've got it covered. Now . . . get ready before I *un*-cover you." He placed a brief kiss on her lips. "I hope you have a costume for tonight."

Alexis bit her lower lip. "*Maybe*," she teased.

Zeke shook his head and walked out the door, mumbling something.

Alexis crawled out of bed when she heard the back door close and turned on the shower. The words "I love you" had been on the tip of her tongue, but she couldn't say them. Not yet. The only other time she professed her love, the relationship had ended. She needed to take another chance at love, because she knew what she wanted, and she wanted Zeke. But it was scary as hell.

She dressed and sent a text to Maggie: *Is it all set?*

Yes. Where r u?

Running late, Alexis typed. *Be there soon. Keep him occupied.* She hadn't thought about a costume, but she knew Maggie could hook her up. She quickly added: *I need a costume.*

K. Three dots appeared again. *You never dress for Halloween.*

She replied with a smiley face and grinned. She was so busted. The permanent smile on her face would give away the delicious, steamy, out-of-this-world night she'd shared with Zeke the minute she appeared on-site.

∼

ALEXIS PULLED to the curb behind Zeke's truck, a smile forming on her lips. She stepped out and pulled her tool belt from the back seat. There was a fresh scent in the air. It would snow tonight; she could feel it. The flurries last night hadn't stuck around, and the ground was barren and crisp. Alexis pulled her canvas coat closed as a gust of north wind sent the remaining brown leaves of an oak tree flittering to the ground.

Thoughts of the cozy flannel sheets on her bed, and notably the man who shared them, warmed her insides.

Zeke waved from the front porch and greeted her when she stepped next to him. The warmth of his lips was brief when he kissed her.

"I'm not sure how we go about this . . . do we tell people?" Zeke asked.

"I think we act normally and let them figure it out on their own. I need to stay professional in front of my crew."

"Understood. Why do you think I snuck out here to wait for you?"

Again, those three words hovered on the tip of her tongue. She needed to pull herself together. She placed a hand on his arm and stepped around him to open the door.

"Hey, Maggie." Her smile broke free once again, and Maggie pulled her out of the room and into the front bedroom. She glanced over her shoulder to see Zeke's eyes glimmer with desire.

"Omigod, Alexis. Tell me everything."

Alexis put a finger to her lips. "Shhh, not here."

Maggie nodded. "Right. I gotcha."

Alexis whispered, "Short answer, yes and epic . . . but that's all you're getting since he's your brother."

Maggie jumped up and down and made the motion of clapping her hands, then hugged her. "It's about time," she quietly stated.

Zeke stood in the doorframe. "Stan has a question about the

tile in the bathroom." He glanced from Alexis to Maggie. With a smirk, he shook his head and left the room.

"Uh-oh." They giggled like schoolgirls and went to talk to the tile setter.

CURIOUS ABOUT WHICH tile Maggie picked, Zeke met the ladies in the master suite. He stepped into the room, where Sean was working on the trim, and noted the smoky gray on two of the walls, and a light ivory color on the rest. "It's looking great in here," he said.

Sean stood and joined him in the center of the room. "I agree. My favorite is the bathtub. The plumber finished up late last night."

Zeke slapped him on the back. "Thanks for staying so I could knock off early."

"Not a problem."

He stepped onto the subfloor and walked toward the large soaker tub. The tile setter stood near the walk-in shower. The closet door creaked behind him, and he turned . . . "Ahhh!" He cursed and jumped out of the way as a skeleton fell into him. He pushed the bones off him, and his hand flew to his heart. The whole house had gathered in the bedroom, and the tile guy shrugged. Alexis and Maggie were bent in half with their hands on their thighs, laughing so hard they were crying.

"Wow. You got me." Zeke's heart still racing, he looked down at the pile of bones. He kicked the skull off his shoe, and it rolled into Alexis.

Their laugh was contagious, which had him laughing along with everyone else. He walked up to Alexis, picked up the skull and held it out in front of him. She heaved in breaths of air as she tried to speak. "You *screamed* . . . like a *girl*."

He whispered in her ear, "Maybe, but I'll enjoy hearing you scream tonight."

She tilted her head, no longer laughing. "Promise?"

Zeke needed to get out of there quick before he tugged her into a closet. "Okay, show's over!"

"Wow, Alexis, I know he's my brother but . . . wow! You could have lit this place on fire with the sparks flying between you two," Maggie said.

"Do you think anyone else noticed?"

"Nah. They all went back to work."

After consulting with the tile setter, they decided the dark gray and light gray tiles looked best in the herringbone pattern in the shower.

"I think you should go with naughty librarian for your costume tonight," Maggie said. "After I'm done here, I'll run home and get a few of my clothing items and set them on your bed. I have the perfect glasses for the ensemble." She glanced over her friend's body. "Yep, I have the perfect skirt, leggings, and shoes. My brother will come unglued when he sees you."

Alexis hoped so. "Thanks, Maggie."

Familiar voices rang out as they entered the kitchen.

"Yoo-hoo . . . anyone here?"

Zeke replaced the baseboard in the living room and stood at the sound of Rosie's voice. His grandma and Emma followed close behind. They each had a bakery box in their hands. "Good morning." Zeke rubbed his hands together in anticipation. "What have you got there?" He placed a kiss on his grandma's cheek.

Emma opened the lid to reveal an assortment of bars and

cookies. "We were next door, delivering goodies to your competition."

Zeke reached into the box and confiscated a frosted brownie. "Do tell." He'd figured his grandma would spy on the other house, and it surprised him it took her this long.

The matchmakers, as Zeke fondly referred to his grandma, her twin, and the owner of the town's only diner, strolled into the kitchen and set the confectionery delights onto the large island. It didn't take long for the rest of the crew to stop for a late-morning break.

"Well," Rosie began, "They were so sweet to show us around. It really will be a beautiful house when they're done."

"Hello, hon," Elsie greeted Alexis and Maggie as they stopped at the counter and peeked into the boxes of goodies. "Alexis, dear, did you do something different to your hair?" Elsie eyed her. "No, that's not it. Are you wearing lip gloss?"

She let go of the box flap and looked at Maggie.

"I think she's glowing," Maggie said and chose a slice of banana bread.

Elsie and Rosie looked to each other and smiled.

Zeke noticed the blush coloring Alexis's cheeks. "Ha! That's probably just sweat," he teased.

"Thanks for the treats. What a lovely surprise." Alexis recovered quickly and chose a Rice Krispies bar.

Zeke's smile widened, showing off his dimple. "These three have been spying on our competition," Zeke announced to take the attention off Alexis. He winked at her.

The women all grinned like a litter of Cheshire cats, but Emma spoke up. "We might have interrupted a little squabble between Ryan and Raven."

"I have to say . . ." Elsie eyed both Zeke and Alexis. "You two are definitely better together."

Zeke had to agree with his grandma. They weren't just better together; they were great together. Why hadn't he seen it before?

James entered the kitchen, camera in hand, and spied the box of treats.

"James, I didn't see you there. Please, come get a treat. How long have you been here?" Zeke asked.

"All morning." James chose a chocolate chip cookie and set his camera on the counter.

Zeke shuffled his feet. "Did you happen to catch the skeleton planted in the closet?"

"Oh yeah. Classic." James chuckled. "Another great outtake for the website."

How did he not see James filming? He glanced in Alexis's direction. Her eyes were as wide as saucers. *Crap.* He'd have to take James aside and find out what else he'd captured on film.

Maggie cleared her throat. "So, tell us what you discovered next door. Do we need to worry?"

James picked up his camera and made for the door. "I can't hear this," he said with a smile at Maggie and the matchmakers. He grabbed another cookie. "Thanks again. Delicious as always."

Elsie, Emma, and Rosie shared with the team that they had nothing to worry about, but they weren't allowed to divulge anything.

Sean walked into the kitchen. "Alexis, the patio door arrived, but they delivered the wrong one."

Elsie pulled Alexis down to her height and placed a kiss on her cheek. "It'll be fine. Don't let anything spoil your glow."

Alexis managed a smile to mask her worry. Not just for the door mix-up, but the possibility of James getting the earlier exchange between her and Zeke on film. "Thanks. I've got to take care of this."

"Go," Elsie said.

Alexis had spent hours on the phone, trying to figure out a

solution, when Zeke came up behind her. "What did you find out?"

"They emailed me a copy of the purchase order, and I'm the one who screwed up." She ran her hand through her hair. "Apparently when I placed the order, I was temporarily dyslexic."

Zeke placed a hand on her shoulder and whispered, "If I could, I'd wrap you in a hug right now. I'd kiss that delectable mouth of yours and run my fingers down your spine. I'd tell you everything will work out."

Alexis met his smoldering eyes and blinked. Words on her lips, she inhaled. "I'd let you hold me and nibble on my neck until I cried out. I'd welcome your strong fingers gliding over my skin . . ."

The sound of a throat clearing made them jump apart and out of their sexual trance. Pete leaned against the doorframe, ankles crossed, with an all-knowing smirk taking up residence on his tired face. "I hope I'm not interrupting anything, General." He nodded. "Zeke."

"No, of course not. Tell me you have a solution." Alexis had called Pete because he had a knack for solving problems that arose on jobsites and had saved her ass many times over the years.

"Yep. It'll only push you back a day. Maybe two."

CHAPTER TWENTY

*A*lexis's mouth hung open at the sight of a sexy pirate costume laid out on her bed.

Phone in hand, she pulled up Maggie's number and placed the call, fingering the white bodice of the costume.

Maggie picked up right away. "I know. I know. Before you say anything, I found out Paige is dressing up as a sexy librarian. I guess it's Ethan's fantasy. *Not* that I needed to know that!"

Alexis waited patiently as Maggie explained and then said, "I can't wear this."

"Why not? You definitely have the body to pull it off."

"I think you mean push it up."

"Potato, Patato."

"Maggie. We're going to a costume party in town."

"So?"

"I have a reputation to uphold."

Maggie let out a giggle. "Well, maybe you'll land more jobs."

"Really? You're seriously going there?"

"Come on, Alexis. Live a little. Besides, I have it on good authority you'll match Zeke."

Alexis sighed. "Is Zeke really dressing as a pirate?"

"Yep. It'll take the pressure off because you're going as a couple. I'm surprised you two didn't coordinate your costumes."

"I didn't decide to go until last night. It isn't high on my priority list." She paused and then gave in. "I'll be the sexy pirate."

"Yeah?"

"Yes. Now I'm hanging up so I can get ready." Alexis ended the call, leaving Maggie cheering on the other end.

UNFORTUNATELY, there wasn't a snowstorm, and the weather was some of the warmest they'd seen on Halloween in a long time. There wouldn't be an excuse for Alexis to wear a bulky winter coat to cover her scarce attire. At least the tall brown leather boots covered most of her legs, the cuffs extending just above the knee.

Alexis entered Zeke's house through the back entrance to avoid the neighbors who had already started their haunts as dusk drew closer.

Zeke whistled and growled, "Delicious!"

Speechless, Alexis smiled at the handsome Jack Sparrow lookalike, who must have been practicing the mannerisms of the famous pirate. Zeke had shaved his recent beard growth into a goatee, somehow adding extra hair with beads. The bandana and dreadlock wig accentuated his badass look. "Did you apply your own makeup? The blue eye shadow and eyeliner look great."

"I did." Zeke pulled a dagger from his side and used the rubber blade to push aside her bodice and expose more of her breast. She moistened her lips, wanting in the worst way for him to undress her.

She grabbed his wrist and brought him in closer. Zeke nuzzled her neck. He whispered in her ear, "You look so hot in your costume. I can't wait to take it off."

Alexis thought maybe she'd get out of this party yet.

The doorbell rang and they reluctantly pulled apart. "That would be Roman and the girls."

She ducked into Zeke's bedroom to adjust her clothing.

ZEKE FLUNG OPEN the door to his twin nieces, Nikki and Nora. "*Arghh*—who goes there?"

"Trick or treat!"

"Well, if it isn't Captain Marvel and Hermione Granger. Very nice!" Zeke ushered the girls inside and placed a black-cat cellophane bag of treats in each of their pillowcases, which matched their costumes. To Roman, he said, "I can't believe you dressed up. It's so unlike you."

"Doesn't he look great? A doctor, just like Uncle Isaiah. We even mussed his hair," Nora said in her best British accent.

"I got to use his stethoscope. I heard my heartbeat," Nikki said.

Nora slugged her sister. "Well I'd hope so, or you wouldn't be walking around now, would you?"

Nikki rewarded her with a karate move, almost kicking the textbook out of Nora's hand. Nora stepped back and raised her wand. "Petrificus totalus."

Roman lowered his voice. "*Girls.*"

Zeke remembered that tone well from when Roman had used it on him as a child.

"I love your costume, Uncle Zeke," Nora said.

"Me too," Nikki said. "I wish I could carry a sword."

Zeke stroked his long, thin wisp of a beard. "I bet you do."

"I'm really glad you can't," Roman said, partly under his breath.

"Hey, everyone. You all look fantastic!"

Everyone's attention focused on Alexis as she entered the

room. Zeke had wondered where she went when the doorbell rang. She was so cute, hiding out. He pulled her in close, wrapping his arm around her waist.

"I love your costume, Alexis!" Nikki said. "Those boots are fire!"

Nora rolled her eyes at her sister. "You look really nice, Alexis."

"Thank you, girls."

Nikki smiled. "I can't wait to wear a costume like that."

"Maybe when you're thirty," Roman said, and Zeke chuckled. Alexis blushed.

"I have to wait until I'm that old? Why?"

They all laughed. Zeke hadn't considered himself old, even if he was pushing thirty.

Nora hugged her textbook and tilted her head. "No, silly, because it's highly inappropriate for someone our age . . . and by the way, Nikki, you have a smudge right here." Nora gestured to the side of her nose. "Did you know?"

"That's Captain Marvel to you."

Roman held back a laugh. "Let's go, girls, your grandma is expecting you."

Nikki and Nora made the rounds of hugs and waved goodbye.

"Have fun, girls," Zeke said and asked Roman, "We'll see you at the lodge later?"

"I'll be there." The girls were halfway down the sidewalk when Roman glanced back at Alexis. "You look beautiful."

"Thank you, Roman."

Roman pulled the door shut, and Zeke moved in close to Alexis. "My brother's right. You look beautiful. Where did you disappear to?"

"Wardrobe malfunction." Her eyes moved down to her breasts.

"Really?"

"I dropped a Junior Mint. It started to melt."

Zeke groaned and grabbed her hand, pulling her toward the bedroom.

"Oh no you don't. We have to go."

Zeke said in his best Johnny Depp impression, "This is the night you will always remember as the night you almost caught Captain Jack Sparrow."

"Don't worry, the night isn't over. Now, the limo will be here any minute."

"Limo?"

"Yep, Owen rented it for the evening so no one has to drive home."

A STEADY STREAM of couples and individuals with creative costumes entered the Blue Ox bar ahead of Alexis and Zeke. They walked through a trail of lighted jack-o-lanterns. They admired several artistic ones along with the ones the family had carved.

Beetlejuice and a good witch dressed in white and pink were collecting the cover charges. "Zeke, you look amazing," said the pretty witch. "You two can go right in. Owen paid for your group already."

Alexis didn't recognize the witch and didn't like how she devoured Zeke with her eyes.

Zeke took Alexis's hand. "Thanks, Abby. Come on, Alexis, Maggie is waving us over."

Alexis's hand covered her mouth when she saw Owen and Maggie. How had she forgotten to ask what the two of them planned to dress as. "Omigosh, you guys!" Alexis had to side-hug Maggie. A landscape oil painting hung from her neck by a blue satin ribbon and covered her torso, but revealed her shapely legs in three-inch white heels and white stockings. "Owen, you're rocking that afro," Alexis said, also noticing the paintbrush and palette he held. She remembered her mom watching Bob Ross on television, teaching the masses how to paint landscapes.

"I told Maggie she could paint my number any time."

Maggie smiled. "The costume was Emma's idea."

Alexis chortled. "I'm pretty sure Bob Ross didn't create paint by numbers."

"Aren't they great!" Paige said as she and Ethan joined the group with drinks in hand.

"You both look amazing too," Alexis said.

Ethan pounded his catcher's mitt. "Yep. I caught my sexy librarian."

"Yes, you did." Zeke leaned over and kissed Paige on the cheek. "Original, bro," Zeke teased Ethan.

"I can still fit into my uniform, so why not? You're rocking the pirate costumes."

"You really are," Owen said.

Maggie sipped her drink through a pink straw. "Totally hot, Alexis, and you too, Jack Sparrow."

Zeke curtsied and pretended to stumble. "What can I get you to drink, my sexy pirate?"

"Just a beer. Any of Garrett's brews."

"Coming right up, my lady." Zeke stroked his long, scraggly beard.

Alexis asked Maggie, "Have you seen Pete? I didn't ask if he planned on coming."

"He's around here somewhere. He rode in the limo with us. There." Maggie pointed at Pete walking toward them in firefighter gear.

"OooEEE, General! You are smokin' hot. I would love to put out your fire."

"Cool it, Pete, or I'll have to hose you off," Alexis said to her good friend.

"Promise? Oh no. I better be good." Pete winked, no doubt spying Zeke at the bar.

"What do you think of my costume?" Pete asked. "Zeke loaned me the uniform." He sported yellow turnout pants and red suspenders.

"I think you have a crowd of women wanting you to put out their fire," Alexis said.

Zeke came up behind Pete and rested a hand on his shoulder.

"Hey, man, thanks for the uniform and wow, great costume," Pete said.

Roman in his scrubs, Cole dressed as Paul Bunyan, and Nick in his sheriff's uniform zigzagged their way toward them, Nick looking annoyed.

"That's either another unoriginal costume or Nick's on duty tonight," Owen said.

"Hey, everyone," Nick greeted them. "Just wanted to say hi before I start my shift."

Owen stood next to him. "You pull the night shift? What about Deputy Dawg?"

Nick grunted. "I can't leave him alone on a night like this. All the troublemakers come out." Nick changed the subject. "I'm glad to find out you all rented a limo for the evening. Smart move. Can you make sure Chloe gets home as well?"

"Yeah, of course. Everyone will have an escort," Owen said.

Nick shook his head.

Owen laughed. "Sorry, man, wrong choice of words."

As if on cue, Chloe meandered over in the most adorable cat costume Alexis had ever seen. Maybe Nick's worries weren't unfounded after all

Nick eyed each woman. "No leaving any drink unattended. If you set your drink down, get a new one."

"Yes, sir." Chloe saluted her brother, and the rest of the group crossed their hearts.

Nick shook his head at Chloe. "Stay safe, everyone. Hopefully I won't be back."

"You too, big brother!" She looked at the girls. "Time to touch up my makeup—who's with me?"

Alexis followed her group of friends to the bathroom. Her ears perked up when she heard Zeke's name, and she slowed her steps to the ladies' room.

"Who do you think is Zeke's flavor of the month?"

The woman in the angel costume had her wings to Alexis, not realizing she was standing behind her, but obviously the wicked witch knew and covered her mouth. Great. Alexis had figured she'd run into one of Zeke's *flavors of the month*. She wanted to rip her wings off.

What was she thinking? Zeke had dated too many women in town, plus he went to high school with most of them. Alexis hurried into the restroom.

Maggie looked at her through the bathroom mirror. "Hey. What's going on, Alexis?"

"Nothing. I'm fine."

Flushing toilets, running water, and a line of costume-clad ladies in front of mirrors touching up their makeup had Alexis turning back toward the door.

"Oh no you don't." Maggie intertwined arms with Alexis and escorted her into the small alcove near the exit door. "Spill."

"Am I Zeke's flavor of the month?"

"What?"

"I overheard a group of women asking who I was."

"Ignore them. My brother might be a flirt, but he only commits to one person at a time. Sounds like they're jealous." Maggie moved in closer. "Hey, look at me. He finally woke up and saw you. He chose you. He has never looked at anyone the way he looks at you."

"It's so new, what if he gets bored?"

"With you? Not a chance. Plus, you've been friends for a long time. Why would he get bored now?" Maggie held her arms open wide. "Come on, bring it in."

They tried to hug, but the oil painting got in their way.

"Oh, for gosh sakes." Maggie flung the canvas around her neck, to her back, and gathered her friend in a huge hug. "Time to have some fun!"

They laughed and joined their friends in the hallway.

"Well, would you look at that," Maggie said.

Alexis, Chloe, and Paige followed Maggie's gaze.

"Well, I'll be," Paige said. "I guess we should have known the women would surround the doctor."

"Do you think we should save him?" Chloe asked. "He looks uncomfortable."

"Well, you are the only one not in a relationship and not family," Paige said.

"Thanks for the reminder."

As they all moved closer to Roman, a genie joined their circle.

"Wow, you're beautiful as a blonde," Alexis said. "Where did you find the costume, Lily?"

"I made it myself. I used to watch reruns of *I Dream of Jeannie*," Lily said and posed with her arms crossed in front of her chest, nodding and blinking the way Barbara Eden had in the show when granting a wish. Her flowing pink costume and bare stomach had all the guys ogling her. "Would you like to make a wish?"

Maggie spoke first. "I wish for you to rescue my brother from Missy Covington and her clan."

"Your wish is my command. Watch and learn, girls."

Alexis, Chloe, Maggie, and Paige practically ran after "Jeannie" to watch the show.

Lily sauntered over and parted the group of tipsy women like the Red Sea, fawning over Roman. She held up her vase and rubbed it. "Well, here I am. What are your other two wishes?" Lily batted her long fake eyelashes at Roman, and Alexis could tell it took him a minute to realize the genie was Lily.

Roman, always the gentleman, held out his arm for her to take, and escorted Lily through the crowd and back to their group of friends.

"That was great. You look awesome, Lily," Roman said. "Thanks for the save."

"Anytime. Plus, I was able to practice my pickup lines."

"Like you need them," Zeke scoffed.

"Oh, but I do. I like to be in control. How about this one . . . Do you know CPR? Because you take my breath away." She winked and took off toward the bar.

Everyone roared with laughter.

"Who knew dressing up like my little brother would attract the women. Isaiah must be turning the ladies away day and night," Roman said.

Paige looked Chloe's way with sympathy. Alexis wondered what that was all about.

"The girls are at Mom's all night, right?" Zeke asked his brother with a knowing grin.

Alexis watched Roman shift slightly, swallow his beer, and ask, "Anyone else need a refill?"

They all raised their glasses. "I'll go with you," Owen said.

Zeke kissed Alexis on the cheek. "I'll help," he said and followed Roman and Owen to the bar.

Lily, with a drink in one hand and her genie bottle in the other, rejoined their group. "Any possible prospects, Chloe?" Lily asked.

"Not really. How about you?"

"No. Most of these guys I've waited on at Rosie's. The others all have dates."

Maggie pointed at the bar. "Alexis? Isn't that Raven?"

Raven, dressed as Elvira, stood too close to Zeke. "Yep. That's her. Excuse me, girls," Alexis said and started for the bar. Raven grabbed Zeke and laid a sensual kiss on his lips.

Alexis stopped and stared, watching the scene unfold in front of her. Zeke grabbed Raven's upper arms and shoved her back. "What the hell?"

Raven placed a finger to her lips and smirked at Alexis. Zeke appeared stunned.

ZEKE WIPED his mouth with the back of his hand and followed Raven's gaze. Furious, he rushed to Alexis.

"That is not what it looked like," he said when he reached her.

"Are you sure? It looked like she ambushed you and you pushed her away."

"Okay, well, yeah." Zeke ran his hand through his dreadlocks. His fingers momentarily got stuck in the wig. "Then I guess it was what it looked like."

"How about we get another drink," Alexis said.

"Yeah?" He gathered her close. "Up for a dance?"

"Sure, but you may want to wash off the bright red lipstick." Alexis pulled a tissue from between her breasts, and he accepted it with a grimace.

"What else do you have in there?"

"Maybe you'll find out later."

Maggie and the rest of Alexis's girlfriends approached them.

"Want me to make her worst nightmare come true?" Lily asked Alexis with evil in her eyes.

"No, It's fine, Lily. She did it to make me angry. I won't let her ruin my night."

~

ALEXIS SEEMED to retreat more and more as the night went on. When she and Zeke arrived back at her house, his phone rang. It took a while to disengage the device from all the layers of his costume. He answered, "This is Zeke."

"Zeke. It's Luke. Is this a bad time?" Alexis had gone into her bedroom to change. He whipped off his wig and placed it on the living room table. "No. What's up?"

"Any chance you could join a few of the guys in Minneapolis for two days? I have a job that pays well. Figured you might want the extra cash for your current project."

Zeke scratched his goatee. "When do I need to be there?"

"By Thursday. You'd be back home by Monday."

Alexis came out of her bedroom, sans makeup and in her pajamas. She glanced at him, sadness in her eyes.

"Luke, I'll call you back." Zeke hung up and went to Alexis.

Her eyes glossy, she said, "I don't think I can do this."

Not understanding, he asked, "Do what?"

She motioned between them. "Us."

"You're kidding, right?" He felt like he had been punched in the gut. "Because of what happened earlier?"

Alexis backed away from him and leaned against the couch. "That and I overheard some of your past conquests ask if I was your flavor of the month."

Anger took over. He widened his stance. "I don't have *conquests*, and I've never had flavors of the month."

"I don't want to be another one of your short-term girlfriends, just to be tossed aside when you get bored."

"That's not fair." Zeke ran his hands through his hair. "What's really happening here?"

Alexis didn't respond.

"You know what? The problem doesn't lie with me. I've always been there for you. I think I've proven that over the years. You're the one who is getting in the way of your own happiness.

Maybe it took me a long time to realize I loved you more than a friend, but my feelings for you are real and unchanging."

Still no response from Alexis. She looked at the floor. Frustrated, he said, "Forget it. You need to figure out what makes you happy. Let me know when you do."

He grabbed his wig and stormed out the door. When he reached his backyard, he pulled out his phone and texted Luke: *I'll be there. Send me the details.*

CHAPTER TWENTY-ONE

With only one week left before the final walk-through and the announcement of the contest winner, Alexis pulled up in front of the Elmhurst house.

Reynolds and Sons landscaping had removed the overgrown bushes and replaced them with new shrubs, and had replaced the broken sidewalk with new concrete. Roman added a dolphin-gray color to the concrete, which complemented the new siding colors: deep blue with charcoal accents and fawn trim. The added roofline supported the new overhang and mission-style columns. The front extension allowed for a covered ramp, which Alexis felt was vital in a Minnesota winter and justified hiring a team from a few counties over to accomplish the task while they were busy on the inside. They'd accomplished a lot in five weeks, more than she'd ever have before, thanks to the support and dedication of the subcontractors and the Hennings' money and influence.

Alexis walked up the ramp and unlocked the mission-style double front door. It was still early, the sun just peeking over the horizon. Her crew was finishing the church remodel, and Maggie was on her way over to start staging. Alexis used to cherish this little slice of alone time, but if she was being honest, she missed Zeke more. He hadn't been home for over a week.

She walked around, viewing the house as if she were a potential buyer. She pulled out her notebook and pen and examined every wall and bit of trim, each register and door, and all the little details she knew a discerning eye would notice. She noted a few scuff marks and places where the paint needed touching up. The scents of fresh paint, wood, and the disinfectant used to wash the floors, countertops, and appliances mixed together to give the house a "new car" smell she enjoyed. The cleaning crew had done excellent work readying the home for the finishing touches, furniture, and all the accessories needed to create the homey feel Maggie was so good at crafting before the cameras arrived.

Her phone pinged with an incoming text from Maggie: *Running late. I'm bringing a truckload and help. See you soon!*

Alexis hadn't slept much. Zeke's sudden departure and their fight played through her mind. She dismissed the memory and texted Maggie back: *No worries.*

Alexis had built her business on her own, and she'd continue to be fine on her own. Her relationship with Zeke had been doomed from the beginning. She'd lost her friend, something she had worried about before allowing her true feelings for him to show.

A large furniture truck pulled to the curb, and Owen jumped out of the passenger side. Maggie followed close behind in Owen's truck, which was full to the brim with boxes. Boxes of what, Alexis didn't know, but knowing Maggie, her creative juices were flowing, and the boxes contained all the finishing touches.

They both waved as Alexis made her way down the sidewalk.

"Help me with these boxes, Alexis, it's all the bedding and linens, vases and knickknacks. There's snow coming our way," Maggie said and shivered. She jumped into the bed of the truck after unloading a dolly and started handing the boxes over the side to Alexis. Alexis loaded the two-wheeler and made several trips inside. When she came out, Owen and a guy she didn't recognize had pulled the ramp out from the truck and started to unload the furniture. Pretty soon, Ethan and Paige showed up, as did Roman and the girls.

While carrying a table into the house, Owen joked, "Where's Zeke? Is he sleeping in or something?"

"Nope. He won't be coming."

Alexis rushed over to the girls to help with a large box and to avoid any more questions about Zeke. She didn't need to start crying in front of Owen.

With the pickup truck unloaded and the furniture in place, Alexis picked up a box marked "master bedroom" and carried it easily through the widened hallway to the largest room in the back. Maggie was there making the bed, and Alexis tried to dump and run, thinking she could retrieve the next box before Maggie could grill her.

"Not so fast. Get in here and shut the door."

"No time, Maggie, we've got a lot to do."

Maggie stood with her hands on her hips. "Where's my brother?"

"How should I know?" Alexis felt her eyes mist, and she turned her head and grabbed a throw pillow from one of the boxes.

Maggie came over and took the pillow from her, placed it back in the box, and wrapped her arms around her. A sob broke loose, and Alexis couldn't stop the tears from falling. Maggie directed her to the bed and they both sat.

"Tell me what happened."

Alexis wiped her flannel-clad arm across her face, took in a deep breath, and hiccupped. "I told him we weren't going to work and that he hadn't changed and that I wasn't ready to be the flavor of the month. He nodded and then accepted a call from Luke. Then he left, saying he had a job and didn't know when he'd be back."

"Why didn't you call me?"

"Nothing to say. He made up his mind, Maggie. We weren't meant to be. I've always been a friend, then lately, a friend with benefits, but it wasn't good enough. I let him loose to explore all the 'angels and witches' out there."

"This is about those women at the costume party?"

Alexis nodded.

Maggie folded her hands on her lap. "I love you, Alexis. But you used those girls as an excuse to distance yourself from Zeke. You're afraid of getting hurt because of what Ryan did to you, and I don't blame you. But don't accuse Zeke of being something he isn't. He waited for you to finish dating the men we set you up with. Why do you think he rescued you from Mitch and took you to dinner? Or stayed with you when you threw out your back? He waited for you to see him, the same way you were waiting your entire life for him to see you. Sometimes love is right in front of you, and you choose not to see it. Sometimes you realize it too late, and sometimes you never see it. In your case, you refused to see it out of fear of being rejected and you pushed Zeke away."

When Maggie had something to say, Alexis knew not to interrupt. "Are you done?" She raised a brow at her friend.

"Yes." Maggie fell back on the bed. "That was a pretty long rant, huh?"

Alexis joined her, looking at the ceiling. "It was good. I needed to hear it."

Maggie patted her leg and stood. She tossed the throw pillows onto the bed. "Here, arrange these pillows."

"Yes, ma'am."

They finished making the bed and placing a few items on the

nightstands in silence until Maggie asked, "So, what are you going to do?"

"No idea. Everything you said was true. I pushed him away. I had hoped he'd fight for me. Instead, he walked away."

"Maybe he's tired of fighting, Alexis. Give him time. Things will work out the way they are intended to. I promise."

By the time Alexis and Maggie were done with the bedroom, the living room furniture had been placed and the other two beds were put together. They had a long night in front of them, but they lived for this stage in a renovation.

Owen had called for pizza, and they ate and talked about the days to come.

"I can't believe you scored all this furniture at the warehouse sale. It actually matches."

Maggie laughed. "Of course it does. Would you expect anything less?"

"No." Alexis threw her arms in the air. "What was I thinking?"

Ethan took a swig from his water bottle and said, "Alexis, this place looks amazing. I especially love the built-ins and the pillars connecting the kitchen and living room."

"I love the short part of the kitchen counter," Nikki said.

Alexis smiled. "I do too. It will be great for someone in a wheelchair. They can sit at the counter and eat or prepare food."

Nikki contemplated her words. "I like that idea."

Roman smiled at his daughter and said, "Alexis, the house is a winner. So many great touches throughout. The Hennings will be pleased."

"Thanks, you guys, that means a lot."

They all tiptoed around the fact Zeke wasn't there, and she appreciated the unspoken words. She knew Maggie had Owen spread the word about not mentioning Zeke's departure.

Alexis hugged each member of Zeke's family and thanked them for all their hard work and for supporting her.

She and Maggie walked back into the house and got to work. They'd have three full days to stage the house. At midnight, Alexis looked at her watch. "Let's call it a night."

Maggie stretched, placing her hands on her lower back. "Sounds good. What time should I be here tomorrow?"

"Enjoy your morning with your husband. I need to stop at the church to check on the progress and talk with Pete. How about ten a.m.?"

"That works."

They both aimed their fobs to remote-start their vehicles. They turned off the lights in the house, locked the doors, and walked through the two inches of snow that had fallen. "You have a great family, Maggie."

"I do. And Alexis, they're your family too."

Alexis hugged her friend, tears threatening. "Good night, Maggie."

"Good night, Alexis."

WITH ALL THE help from family and friends, the staging only took two days instead of three.

Out of habit, Alexis checked her phone. She wished Zeke would text her. She entered her home and Boo rubbed against her leg, his purrs vibrating through the quiet house. Alexis removed her shoes and hung up her coat. She placed her hat and gloves in the galvanized bin in the foyer and headed for the fridge. "Let's get you something to eat." Alexis pulled the can of cat food from the fridge and emptied it into Boo's dish. She placed the fork in the sink, pulled a box of Junior Mints from the cupboard, and headed to the bedroom to change into her pajamas. She and Maggie had finished the staging. They'd met their deadline.

When she crawled into bed and pulled the covers over herself, they smelled of Zeke. Boo settled next to her as she cried herself to sleep.

∽

THE NEXT MORNING, Alexis woke to a text message. Startled out of a deep sleep, she reached for her phone, but she knocked it across her nightstand and it landed on the floor. Boo, alert after being jostled from sleep, jumped off the bed and attacked the phone like it was a rodent trying to escape. Flinging the covers back, Alexis bolted out of bed and rescued her device from the kitten. Her heart plummeted when the text was from Kate and not Zeke.

She pulled up the text and read: *Hi, Alexis. I wanted to let you know I decided to stay in Chicago for Thanksgiving. I'll be arriving on Black Friday.*

Alexis typed a reply: *Your home will be ready when you get here. I'll keep the lock box on the door. The code is 4167. Call or text when you arrive, and I can meet you there if you'd like.*

Three dots appeared, indicating Kate was typing. Boo had jumped back on the bed and was attacking the string on her pajama bottoms.

Kate's response appeared: *I'm excited!*

Alexis picked Boo up and carried him into the kitchen. She set him down in front of his bowl and opened a can of food. After Boo was fed, she made coffee.

Boo followed her into the bedroom, where he wrestled with every piece of clothing she set on the bed. Alexis smiled at his antics. She walked over to the T-shirt Zeke had discarded in haste the last time he was there. She picked it up and brought it to her nose. Should she send him a text? Try to call him?

No. He had taken a job for Luke. She dressed and headed for the church to let Pete know he had an extra week.

～

"HI, PETE."

Pete walked right to her and wrapped her in a hug. "I never did like him."

Alexis smacked him. "Yes you did."

She loved the support, but it was her fault Zeke walked away. When they pulled apart, Alexis shoved her hands into her front pockets and looked down at the floor. "He didn't do anything wrong, Pete. I pushed him away. My insecurities surfaced."

Pete removed his tool belt, and they sat on two overturned buckets. "What are you going to do about it, General?"

"I don't know. Maggie said it'll work out the way it's intended to, but I need to do something. I need to reach out to him."

"Have you tried calling him?"

"No. He's on a job. I don't want to distract him."

"General, if it were me, I'd already be distracted thinking about you. He's crazy about you. Call him. Leave him a message. Tell him how you feel. Tell him you're sorry. Tell him you love him." Pete knocked shoulders with her. "Don't try denying it. You love him, he loves you—it's not rocket science. Spill your guts and then leave it up to him."

"When did you get so in touch with your feelings?"

"Oh, please. I grew up with five older sisters. They talked about their feelings all the time."

"Thanks, Pete. I'll take your advice. But first, I have some news that should make your day."

Alexis looked around at Kate's living space, which still

needed painting and trim work. "You have another week. Kate won't arrive until Black Friday."

"That is good news. The extra week will help."

Alexis's phone dinged. A text from Ryan: *Can we meet?*

Pete glanced at her phone. "Wonder what that's about."

"I don't know and don't want to know."

"You're not going to text him back?"

"Nope."

Her phone dinged again: *Please? We should talk.*

"You know, Ryan isn't a bad guy," Pete said. "He's an idiot for doing what he did to you, but you two were never right together anyway."

"What? Why didn't you say anything?"

"Not my place. Besides, would you have listened?"

"No. I guess not." Alexis shoved him. "I would have thought you were jealous and I'd need to let you down easy, saying we could only be friends."

Pete's loud guffaw echoed through the building. "All kidding aside, I think you need the closure that Ryan can give you before you can move on with your life."

Geez, why did everyone think she needed unsolicited advice? She picked up her phone and texted Ryan back: *Tonight? The Blue Ox. 7:30?*

She looked at Pete. "Happy?"

Ryan responded: *Sounds good. I'll be in the bar. Thanks.*

ALEXIS HAD one goal after accepting Ryan's invitation—get in and get out as quick as possible.

She'd been in a funk since the fight with Zeke, and she didn't feel like dressing the part of the successful contractor. In fact, she didn't feel successful at the moment, with now two failed relationships. She didn't go home and change; she had no one to impress. Alexis didn't care what Ryan thought of her. She wasn't Raven, dressed to the nines at a jobsite, and never would be.

Scanning the parking lot, she noticed Ryan's emblemed truck and pulled into the open space next to him. With all the energy she could muster, she climbed out of her truck and glanced at her image in the large side mirror. Dark circles had formed under her eyes. Running a hand through her hair, she tucked one side behind her ear and entered the bar.

The Blue Ox patrons were mostly vacationers who stayed at the Deer Creek Lodge. Moody blues played over the speakers, and the lights were dim. Alexis walked into the bar and scanned the area for Ryan. She found him sitting alone at the far end of the large walnut bar. She hadn't planned to meet him while he was in town and had gone out of her way to avoid any contact. Maybe it was good that Pete had made her change her mind. The winner would be announced at the end of the week, and she and Ryan would probably never cross paths again. Did she hope for an apology? She did. He'd hurt her in ways she hadn't realized until she sabotaged the only relationship she really cared about. Pete said she needed closure to move on. She hoped to get some.

She pulled out a barstool and sat. "Hi."

"Hey." Ryan rubbed his jaw. "Thanks for meeting me."

Alexis nodded and signaled for the bartender. "Sure."

The bartender placed a coaster advertising Garrett's brewery. "A Loon Call Lager, please," she said.

"Coming right up."

The bartender set her beer down.

"Thanks." She took a sip. "So, I'm here. What's so important that we need to meet?" She might have had a little too much snark in her tone, but Ryan didn't seem to take offense.

"First, I want to sincerely apologize for the way we ended. I regret what I did to you."

"Yeah, it wasn't your finest moment." Alexis took another swig, needing liquid courage.

Ryan rubbed his jaw again. She remembered this nervous gesture of his.

"I didn't ask you here to bring up the past or to offer excuses for my behavior, but I needed to say I'm sorry," he said.

"I appreciate that." She played with the label on the bottle, keeping her eyes forward, looking at him in the mirror above the bar. She waited for him to continue.

"I met with James and Susan before calling you and told them I was withdrawing from the contest. Even if I did win—although I'm pretty sure I don't have a chance—I wouldn't have the time to take on a large project like the Whitmore Estate."

"Wait—" She swiveled her bar stool to face him, and Ryan did the same, their knees knocking.

Ryan shifted slightly so as not to invade her space. "Let me finish. It has nothing to do with you. The contest has brought us a lot of publicity. A real estate developer called and asked if I would be his exclusive contractor. I'm meant to build new. Your passion is remodeling, and you've got the talent to bring the old back to life."

Alexis relaxed into the high-back leather stool. "Wow. Congratulations, and thanks." She paused and surprised herself by realizing she actually meant it. "Can I ask you something?"

"Sure."

"Why did you participate in this contest, living so far away?"

"I heard you'd be the other builder, and I wanted to see if you might give *us* another chance." He looked down at the bar.

She snorted but didn't mean to . . . mostly. "Sorry, that was rude." He really thought she'd take him back?

"No need to apologize. When you walked up to the fence line the first day, you walked with such confidence. You stole my breath away, just like you did the first time you arrived on my jobsite. But when I noticed your electrician, I knew I didn't have a chance."

"Zeke?"

"Yeah. He looked like he was ready to take a swing at me if I said the wrong thing, and then I noticed the way you looked at him. I knew I had blown a good thing. Besides, you never looked at me the way you look at him."

Alexis didn't know what to say. She took another drink and glanced at the game playing on the screen above the bar. The Eagles scored a touchdown against the Packers. "Are you expecting me to thank you for relinquishing the job?"

"Nope. I saw your house; you deserve the win. I wish I hadn't blown it with you." Ryan tapped her thigh, stood, and threw cash on the bar. "Take care, Alexis."

"You won't be at the party tomorrow?"

"I'll be there for the announcement."

She watched Ryan walk away. She'd gotten the Whitmore and saved her business. So why did she feel like such a failure?

CHAPTER TWENTY-TWO

*A*lexis paced like a caged animal, wearing a path in her kitchen floor. Boo watched from one of the kitchen chairs until finally he tired of her movements and fell asleep. She needed to call Zeke. Would he answer? Ignore her call? Or would he tell her she wasn't worth the trouble?

Her heart skipped a beat when a text came in. It was from Susan. Her shoulders relaxed. Not Zeke. *James and I will meet you, Maggie, and Zeke at the house at two this afternoon. I can't wait! I'm so excited to see what you've done.*

Alexis glanced at the clock above her kitchen window. She had six hours to reach Zeke and see if he'd meet them at the house.

Here goes nothing, she thought. She dialed his number and waited.

Zeke's deep voice said, "Hello?"

"Hi." She rushed on. "I'm not sure if you're in town, but I need to talk to you. Is this a good time?"

"Sure, Alexis. It's good to hear your voice."

Surprised and elated, she continued, "I'm sorry, Zeke. I let fear dictate my actions. I know I don't deserve another chance, but I sure hope you'd consider letting me explain and show you how much I love you."

"You . . . love me?"

"Yes. I've been in love with you since we were teenagers."

"Wow. I wish I had known. I was kind of an idiot back then."

"It's probably better that you didn't know. I think we needed to go through the experiences we did in order to appreciate each other now."

"Then it's a good thing."

"What is?"

"That I rushed back to be with you."

The kitchen door opened, and in walked Zeke, sexy as ever with his hair mussed and his goatee still gracing his strong jaw— minus the added beads from his Jack Sparrow costume.

Their phones still to their ears, they stepped closer together.

"So, you love me, huh?" Zeke's dimple was on full display.

Alexis pressed end, placed her phone on the island, and walked into his outstretched arms.

He whispered into her ear, "I love you too. I couldn't wait to get home."

ZEKE KISSED the crown of Alexis's head as she rested it against his chest. "I shouldn't have left, but when Luke called and asked me to take one last security assignment involving Mandy Blake, I was torn. Mandy was nervous and asked for me."

Alexis stepped back. "So, are you going to run off whenever Mandy Blake needs to feel secure?"

Zeke took her hands in his, "No. In fact, she's actually a romantic at heart and encouraged me to come back to Deer Creek Falls and fight for you. Not that I needed any encouragement."

"You didn't?"

"I will always run back to you no matter where I am. Please

believe me when I tell you she and I never had anything going on. She was my client, and that's all she'll ever be. Besides, I would never have heard the end of it if I didn't come back and make things right with you."

"How so?"

"I had calls from both Maggie and Ethan telling me how disappointed they were in me."

"They didn't." Alexis grinned.

Zeke nodded.

Alexis seductively unbuttoned her plaid shirt and shrugged her arms out of the sleeves. Zeke rushed forward, their mouths connected in a frenzy of kisses, and he carried Alexis to the bedroom.

ALEXIS STOOD NEXT TO ZEKE, looking at the Elmhurst house. "How do you feel?" Zeke asked.

"You mean about earlier or about the house?" She smiled.

"I know how you felt earlier." He hugged her close.

"I'm pleased at what we've accomplished."

He planted a kiss on her temple. "I'm sorry I wasn't here for the final touches."

The Hennings arrived at the same time Maggie pulled into the drive. A smile formed on Maggie's face when she noticed Zeke and Alexis's hands intertwined.

"Good to see you, Zeke," James said.

"Good to be here."

Susan hugged everyone. With all the greetings out of the way, she stood back and spread her arms wide. "Wow. I've been dying to drive past the houses but refrained. It wasn't easy! I can't believe this is the same house. The covered porch is beautiful. I could look at it all day, but it's cold out here. Let's go inside."

169

James had the camera on his shoulder, and Maggie stood by Alexis's side. Zeke held Alexis's hand. She took a deep breath. "Yes. I hope you're pleased," she said.

The four of them walked up the ramp, and Zeke held the door open for James.

"Oh my! Alexis . . ." Susan covered her mouth. Her eyes darted around the living room, which was now open to the kitchen.

"Wasn't there a wall here?"

Zeke squeezed Alexis's hand and nodded, urging her to give the tour and point out the hidden treasures of the home. She smiled at Zeke before saying, "Yes. The rooms were small. Too small for someone in a wheelchair to get around . . ."

When the tour was over, they all gathered around the kitchen island. James handed Alexis an envelope. She didn't need to open it to know it was the final payment. She simply pocketed it and said, "Thank you. I hope you're pleased with the results."

"I am. Excellent work." He glanced at Zeke and Maggie. "All of you."

"Are you ladies buying a new dress for the reveal party? I already found the perfect outfit at Chloe's darling shop," Susan said.

"I already set mine aside. Chloe's making me a necklace for it as we speak," Maggie said.

Alexis glanced at Maggie. "Well, I guess I better get over there."

"Are you excited, Alexis?" Susan asked. "Only two days until the big reveal."

"I am."

James wanted to shoot more footage of the house, so the rest of them left.

"Can I steal Alexis away for the evening, Zeke?" Maggie asked.

Zeke grumbled, "Only if you bring her back to me."

Maggie grinned from ear to ear. "Of course."

"What do you have in mind, Maggie?" Alexis asked.

"We're heading to Chloe's for some girl time and to celebrate."

Although girl time sounded wonderful, she wasn't ready to leave Zeke so soon. She looked to him for his opinion.

"Go. Have fun. I'll be at your house when you get there. If you need a ride home, call."

"Are you sure?"

"Yeah, I need some Boo time. I missed the little guy."

She kissed him on the lips, intending it to be a quick peck, but they got carried away.

Maggie cleared her throat. "Okay, you two. Break it up."

WHEN ALEXIS and Maggie arrived at Chloe's, all the girls were waiting for them.

"Spill. You kissed and made up?" Lily said.

Zeke had put a permanent smile on Alexis's face. "Yes. It's official. No more hiding our feelings from each other or my crew. I was stupid."

Maggie reached for her hand. "No you weren't, you were scared. Believe me, we've all been there."

Chloe, Lily, and Paige all nodded as they made their way to the living room. "I've never seen Zeke this happy before. I reminded him never to let you go," Paige said.

"Wait. How did you all find out?"

"You haven't seen the post?" Chloe asked.

"No–oo. Town Talk?"

The girls all smiled. Chloe lifted herself off the couch and walked over with her phone in hand. "It's all right here." She handed Alexis the phone.

Alexis's eyes misted over, and her smile widened. The post read "My one and only." Zeke had posted a picture of them he had taken at the Lakeside Inn.

"When was that picture taken?" Lily asked.

Alexis laughed. "During my second date, well . . . After my date with Mitch, Zeke rescued me. Technically our first official date."

She had so much to tell the girls, so she started at the beginning. They laughed so hard they cried. Maybe it was the brandy slushes, or maybe it was the stress relief they all needed.

Alexis had missed the camaraderie with her girlfriends. Asking for help never came easy for her. She'd learned that relying on other people wasn't a weakness; sometimes it was necessary. Her friends helped her see that, and she thanked them for their continued love and support.

CHAPTER TWENTY-THREE

*Z*eke wiped his sweaty palms on his worn jeans. The details were set. The plans in motion. The frozen ground crunched under his rubber-soled work boots as he exhaled puffs of air the way his granddad used to with his pipe. He took the first step and climbed. When he reached the top, he rested his forearms on the railing and breathed in the frigid air. A covering of ice had formed on Balsam Bay, and across the water, the sugar maples stood statuesque, barren of their leaves on this calm morning. Zeke felt anything but calm. He chose truth over fear and hoped he played his cards right.

He sent a text to Maggie: *All set.*

Rewarded with a half dozen smiley face emojis, his smile widened, his heart full.

The idea had formed when watching Alexis's interview on the contest house. Contacting Garrett was his first step to making his plan a reality. His good friend, an architect, enjoyed the challenge, as did his brother Ethan and brother-in-law, Owen. Cole, a master woodworker, had also lent a hand, and the result was phenomenal.

ALEXIS HADN'T BEEN able to get a hold of Zeke all day. He'd left to take care of something and said to meet him at Ethan's. She sent a quick text to Zeke before this whole fourth-date thing blew up in her face: *Maggie arranged for a new guy to meet me at Ethan's get-together tonight. Not my idea. I can't imagine what she was thinking.*

Zeke still hadn't responded as she pulled on her black lace bra and panties and dressed in a turtleneck sweater, jeans, and leather boots. It wasn't like he hadn't already seen everything in her wardrobe, because it wasn't extensive unless you counted the multitude of flannel shirts and well-worn jeans. But she wanted to wear something he had admired.

She picked up her phone and noticed a missed call, then a text from Maggie. *Change of plans*, the text read. *Please call me before you leave.*

Alexis punched in Maggie's number, and the phone connected with her friend's hurried voice. "Have you left yet?"

"Nope. Sorry I missed your call. I was getting dressed and my phone was in the kitchen."

"Okay, good. Can you drive to my house? I'll explain when you get here."

"Okay. I'm leaving now. See you soon."

Maggie usually extended her goodbyes, but this time she simply hung up. Something wasn't sitting right. Alexis hoped it didn't have anything to do with the new guy she'd meet tonight. Maggie had promised she would warn the guy that Alexis and Zeke were an item and that there would no longer be any kind of a date. Alexis chose her black leather jacket with faux-fur collar and set out toward Maggie and Owen's place.

When she pulled into the driveway of the Reynolds family homestead, now Maggie and Owen's home, she noticed Maggie jumping up and down to stay warm while texting. What on earth was she doing waiting outside?

Alexis climbed out of her truck, and Maggie ran up to her.

"Why are you outside? I would have knocked," Alexis chastised her friend.

"I know. Come on. I need your help. I have something at my old cabin I need to bring to Ethan's."

"So, we're walking over?" Alexis looked at her best friend bundled to the hilt in cold-weather gear. With her cute headband and matching mittens, her outfit screamed "adorable snow bunny."

"Yeah. Will you be warm enough? I have extra mittens."

"Nope, I'm good. Let me grab my headband and gloves from the truck." She turned and reached into the cab. "Okay, I'm ready," she said, pulling them on.

"Great." Maggie, clearly involved in texting someone, quickly stored her phone in her jacket pocket. Her smile hinted that she was up to no good.

The resort in winter reminded Alexis of a magical fairy tale. The snowflakes that had fallen this morning were now glistening in the beams of light from the cabins. "So, are you going to tell me what's going on?"

Maggie stopped at cabin twelve, where she had lived before she and Owen bought the family home. "I don't know what you mean."

Out of the corner of her eye, Alexis noticed a man walking out of the woods. Not just any man, but the man she couldn't get enough of. How had she not noticed the trail of lights leading through the woods? She stood frozen in place.

ZEKE CAME to a stop in front of Alexis and his sister, but his focus was all on Alexis, the woman he wanted in the worst way. "Hi."

"Hi," Alexis said.

"Well, that's my cue to leave."

Zeke heard the words Maggie spoke but didn't comment, then heard Maggie's footsteps crunching on the snow behind him as she walked toward Ethan's place. He reached out for Alexis's gloved hand. He gently tugged and nodded toward the illuminated trail. "Come with me."

"Aren't we going to Paige and Ethan's?" Alexis sucked on her lower lip, and all his attention was drawn to her mouth.

"Yes. But I have a surprise for you."

Zeke cupped her face and kissed her. Feeling the warmth of her lips, his insides and extremities heated. He pulled back and gazed into her glacial blue eyes. "Do you trust me?"

"I do."

He smiled at her choice of words, took her hand, and led her through the pine trees, holding her close to his warm body.

"Zeke, I thought maybe we could ditch everyone and enjoy some alone time. I hoped maybe we could go back to your place." When Zeke didn't respond, she hurried on. "Did you get my text? Did Maggie explain about date number four?"

He looked down at her and kissed her forehead. "I'm well aware of date number four. I want to show you something first."

She giggled. "I've already seen it."

Alexis was his one. She made him laugh. "Well, yes you have, but I have a different surprise for you. Although I think the latter could be arranged."

He knew the minute she noticed the incredible treehouse. She stopped and squeezed his hand, her eyes wide open.

With the help of his friends and family, he had organized the building of the treehouse in record time. Tears streamed down Alexis's face as she moved closer to the string of lights that shone on the carved sign at the stairway entrance. The sign read "KEEP OUT," and in the bottom corner, their initials, ZR plus AW, were surrounded by a heart.

. . .

ALEXIS WIPED AT HER TEARS, her eyes blurry. She removed her glove and traced the heart. She looked to Zeke for answers.

"How did you know?"

"How would I not know? We've been friends a long time. So, you like it?"

"You mean the amazing fortress high in the trees? The sign? Or the sexy, handsome, loving, and kind man in front of me?"

Alexis wrapped herself around him. "I love you, Zeke Reynolds."

After she released him, he said, "Follow me."

Following Zeke up a set of stairs, across a short rope bridge, up another set of steps, and to the door of the treehouse took longer than it probably should. She inspected every detail, taking in the hardware used, the wood, and the steel roof. This was the best gift she had ever received.

He pushed the door open and gestured for her to go in first. A large, round, dark-chocolate-colored floor cushion the size of a bed held multiple throw pillows in shades of cream. Alexis removed her gloves. The room was warm. She looked around for the heat source and noticed a heater that gave off serious BTUs. Everything about the treehouse was top of the line. Zeke removed his jacket and hung it on a peg by the door, then helped her out of hers.

He rolled the sleeves of his white dress shirt up to his elbows, showing off his muscular forearms. He wore faded jeans and black boots. Her mouth watered with the anticipation of undressing him slowly in this amazing treehouse.

She sputtered, "How? When?"

"The past few weeks."

Alexis began to protest, and he silenced her with a finger to her lips.

A corner of his mouth quirked up. "It pays to have a brother-in-law who owns one of the largest hardware store chains in the country and has the resources to get the job done quickly."

"Maybe I should have had Owen help me when I was trying to find another crew."

Zeke pulled her in close. "You weren't willing to accept help at that point."

"True."

Before she knew what was happening, Zeke was down on one knee with a velvet box held out in front of him.

"Alexis. I may have taken a while to realize what was in front of me, but when I did, I fell for you hard and fast. I love you and want to spend my life with you. I'm better with you, we're better together, and I want to show you that every day for the rest of our lives. Will you marry me?"

Alexis kept her focus on Zeke. "Yes. I want that more than anything. I love you, Zeke Reynolds."

Zeke slid the platinum-and-diamond band on her finger and sprang to his feet, engulfing her in his embrace. He pulled back and reached for a small metal box with a red button. "Here, push this."

She eyed him suspiciously and pushed the button, wondering if it did anything, and then they heard the cheers and applause outside. He wrapped his hand around hers, and they walked outside onto the small deck to see the Reynolds clan smiling up at them. Zeke pointed at the cloth hanging over the railing, which had unfurled at the push of the button. Alexis looked over the edge and read the sign upside down. It read "She said yes!"

Elsie, Abe, Linnie, Roman, Nikki, Nora, Ethan, Paige, Maggie, and Owen all shouted various salutations.

Maggie called up, "You sure took your time, Zeke. We're all freezing out here."

Then Elsie yelled, "Don't listen to Maggie. We'll leave you two alone to enjoy your new fort." When the matriarch of the family spoke, the rest of them obeyed and headed back to Ethan's without another word.

Back in the warmth of the treehouse, Alexis asked, "Is this going to be a family treehouse?"

Zeke pulled her down onto the round bed. "Heck no. This is our place."

"How?"

"I had it built on my property."

"Your property?"

"Yep. When Ethan came home, he purchased the entire parcel from the resort to just past his place. He sold me the middle parcel after he built his house. That way, when I decided to settle down with a family of my own someday, I'd have land to build the perfect house."

She smiled at him, her lips a breath from his. "Is this your idea of our perfect house?"

"For now. Until we build something together."

"Then this is our love shack?"

Zeke fell back laughing and pulled her on top of him. "I like that idea. It's warm and well insulated." He winked.

Between kisses, Alexis asked, "What about my fourth date—I kind of feel bad for standing him up."

Zeke laughed. "Maggie and I set this up." He pushed the hair from her eyes and tucked it behind her ear. I'm your fourth date . . . and the last one you'll ever need."

CHAPTER TWENTY-FOUR

*A*lexis stood next to Zeke backstage at the high school, their hands clasped together, her engagement ring sparkling in the lights. A calm settled over her. The camera no longer made her nervous. When Ryan had surrendered the Whitmore remodel, she'd rested easier, but it was more than that, that made her calm. The fact that she could continue doing what she loved to do, and with the love of her life next to her, made all the difference in the world.

"Hey, it's going to be fine," Zeke said.

"I know. I'm not scared anymore."

"You're not? There's a big crowd out there."

"Well, I was okay . . ." she said and giggled as he pulled her into his arms.

"Hey, sorry I'm late." Maggie came bounding up behind them. "Chloe and James are filming the crowd. We have a full house. I even heard some people say they drove from Michigan to witness the win." Alexis glanced around for Ryan. She spotted him making his way through the stage door. She squeezed Zeke's hand.

"I didn't think you were going to make it," she said as Ryan approached.

"I had to take care of something."

"Where's Raven?" Maggie asked.

"She's not coming. I asked her not to join me onstage after hearing about what she pulled." Ryan extended a hand to Zeke. "Sorry about Raven's behavior."

"No worries. She didn't ruin anything." Zeke raised their clasped hands to show Ryan the ring.

"I guess congratulations are in order."

Alexis wasn't sure how to respond so she simply said, "Thank you."

A voice rang out over the sound system. "Testing one two three . . . testing. Good evening. Thank you for coming. My name is Susan Henning, director of Shaping Our Future non-profit. My husband James and I started Shaping Our Future to give back to the community where we've decided to live out our retirement."

Okay, maybe Alexis's nerves weren't as steady as she thought. The four of them focused on Susan.

"We've lived in five countries and dozens of cities, but never have we felt so welcomed as we have since we chose to purchase our home in Deer Creek Falls. Community means something different to all of us, and we belong to many communities that nurture us in different ways. Your community may be your yoga class, a book group, a coffee club, or game night with friends. Each welcoming and supportive. Belonging and working toward a common goal, encouraging one another and challenging each other, is what matters most. We created a challenge as you all have read about on our small town's website, some of which will be published in the *Remodelers Platform* online magazine.

"Tonight, we come together to celebrate two builders whose renovations will make life easier for veterans recuperating from injuries sustained while serving our country. Thanks to these brave individuals, we can feel safe in our communities."

Alexis wiped her sweaty palms along her sweater dress and smiled at Zeke. He kissed her temple and drew her in close. She wondered when Susan would wrap up her speech and get on with the announcement.

"We've received more response than we ever imagined from our little contest." Susan glanced at the index card in her hand. "In total, 103,017 people voted for the winning house, but before I announce the winner—and both teams are winners in my book —let's meet them. Please welcome Ryan Anderson of Harmony Construction."

Ryan walked onto the stage with a hand raised to the crowd. There were cheers and a few whistles. Images of the house he remodeled appeared behind him on a large screen, the slideshow looping through the rooms.

Susan continued, "Now, please welcome Deer Creek's very own Alexis Welby of Do-Over Renovations and her designer, Maggie Jacobs."

Maggie grabbed Alexis's hand and raised it high as they joined Ryan onstage. The crowd cheered, hooted, and hollered, and Ryan clapped for them too.

Alexis and Maggie shifted slightly to look at the slideshow behind them.

"As you all know, the contest was created to allow my husband and I to choose between our favorite contractors to remodel our new home. Although that is still the case, these indi- viduals"—Susan gestured to the three of them onstage—"created beautiful accommodations for our veterans, and we couldn't be prouder of their abilities and their visions for these homes. So, without further ado, the online survey results are . . ."

Susan tore into the white envelope. Her eyebrows rose and she smiled. "This is very close."

Everyone looked around, waiting for the results. Alexis squeezed Maggie's hand.

"Congratulations, Alexis Welby of Do-Over Renovations, winning by a close margin of 713 votes!"

Alexis hugged Maggie, and she could hear Pete yelling from the crowd, of course using her nickname. The Reynolds family made their way toward the front of the crowd, and Zeke ran out from backstage. Ryan offered his congratulations and said goodbye to James and Susan.

Even though Alexis had already known she'd be the contractor on the Whitmore Estate, winning the contest justified her hard work and long hours. Zeke lifted her off her feet and swung her around. When he set her down, her mom, Pete, and the Reynolds family surrounded her in a large group hug.

EPILOGUE

$\mathcal{T}$he Whitmore Estate sat on a hill overlooking Balsam Lake. When Zeke and Alexis pulled into the circular drive, a valet opened their door. White lights adorned the stone steps. Pumpkins, gourds, ornamental cabbage, and cornstalks flanked the large wooden door. The couple of inches of snow they'd gotten earlier in the week remained on the ground. The stars lit the night sky, making the evening magical.

Zeke and Alexis walked hand in hand up the stone steps. They, along with half the town, had been invited to a catered dinner and celebration at the majestic old home.

"Just think how beautiful this place will be once you and Maggie dig in," Zeke said.

"Don't you mean when *we* get our hands on this property?"

Zeke kissed her temple. An exuberant Susan answered the door. "You made it!"

"Of course. We wouldn't miss it," Alexis said as she took in the space around her.

"Come in, come in. The food is in the ballroom. Let me take your coats. Please make yourselves at home. I'll be right back. I

184

need to speak with James." Susan hurried off in search of her husband.

"Wow," Zeke said as he turned in a circle, taking in the open foyer. The dark wood beams and floors had seen better days, but were still grand.

"I know." Alexis walked to the staircase and ran her hand along the banister. "These stairs make me think a princess in a beautiful gown will make an entrance at any minute."

Zeke wrapped his arms around her from behind and nuzzled her neck. "Why Alexis, I never knew you were the fairy-tale princess type."

"Zeke, all women dream of their Prince Charming." She turned and interlaced her arms around his neck. "I'm one of the lucky ones. I found my prince."

"Hey, you two, break it up. You're making me blush," Ethan said, carrying a plate of food piled high. "You have to try the food. The stuffed mushrooms and crab cakes are mouthwatering."

Zeke rubbed his stomach and it grumbled. "I'm starving. I worked up an appetite." He winked at Alexis.

Alexis blushed and waved to Paige. She joined them, holding a plate of food that smelled delicious.

Nick joined them too. "Great job on the house, Alexis. I can't wait to see how you'll bring life into this old place."

"Thanks, Nick. Congratulations on officially becoming sheriff. You were the right man for the job."

Nick laughed. "I guess, seeing as I ran uncontested."

"Alexis, you have to try the mushrooms," Paige said. "Let's leave these guys to talk amongst themselves. Come with me. The girls are in the ballroom."

Alexis kissed Zeke on the cheek. "Duty calls."

Maggie approached her at the buffet table. "I already went on a tour. Susan and James had all the furniture they are keeping moved to the third floor. She told me the attic is full of treasures and to come and explore. I can't wait to get my hands on the vintage pieces. I'm hoping I can salvage some things to incorporate into the remodel."

"This is going to be great, Maggie." Alexis spied Pete talking with the Reynolds brothers. "Did Pete tell you?"

Maggie's face lit up. "You mean, that he's decided to stay?"

"Yes! Of course he told you. Does he plan to continue renting a cabin from you?"

"For now. But if I'm right, he'll look for something more permanent," Maggie said.

"Yeah, that's the vibe I got from him too. When Brad called and told me he and his wife decided on him being a stay-at-home dad, I asked Pete to stay on as my foreman, and he jumped at the chance."

Susan and James strode into the ballroom hand in hand, with Zeke following behind. "Alexis," James said, "we'd like to discuss something with you and Zeke. Let's go into the library."

"Okay." She glanced at Zeke, and he shrugged his shoulders. She handed her plate to Maggie. "I'll be right back."

It didn't go unnoticed that she and Zeke left the room with their hosts, because when they stepped back into the ballroom, everyone eyed them with curiosity. Their friends and family noticed the smiles on their faces.

James tapped his wine glass with a silver knife, and his booming voice rang out, "Can I get everyone's attention, please?"

The room quieted instantly.

"I'd like to make an announcement. I just informed Alexis and Zeke I sent some footage of them remodeling the home to a producer friend of mine."

Soft jazz played in the background, and feet shuffled closer to hear.

"My contact offered them a chance at a syndicated show. A program to showcase their town. Our town." He looked to his wife with a smile on his face. "The first house they'll remodel together will be the Whitmore. It will be the pilot that will determine whether the producers pursue the television series."

Gasps were heard, and cheers erupted.

"WELL, I'LL BE!" Rosie said. "Doesn't that just beat all."

Elsie hugged Emma. "We did it again, ladies."

Rosie sipped from her glass of champagne, "I have to admit, Elsie, your idea of encouraging the ladies to set Alexis up on those dates was genius. Making Zeke jealous was the kick in the pants he needed."

"Here's to another successful match, and what a wonderful opportunity for our small town. Cheers!"

Elsie held her hand out to her daughter, Linnie, when she approached their table.

"Well, Mom? Who's next?"

"Whatever do you mean, dear?" Elsie eyed her daughter.

Linnie laughed as Ruth Reid joined them, and they both sat.

"Yes, ladies," Ruth said. "Who's next on your radar? Linnie now has two of her children on the way to the altar and one already married. My boys have yet to bring home a woman to meet us. Nick is always working, Garrett is too busy opening a second location of his brewery, Cole isn't showing any interest, and neither is his sister. I really want some grandbabies."

Emma patted Ruth's hand. "Well. I heard the council hired a new deputy. It's a woman . . . and Kate Davis, the owner of the coffee shop, will be arriving soon. Two women are joining our small town. There is hope for your good-looking boys. I can feel it in my old bones."

Ruth smiled, held up her glass, and said, "Cheers to our single children, who sometimes need a little extra nudge in the love department."

A chorus rang out. "Hear, hear!"

Elsie took a sip of wine. "Ladies, I believe Nick is next. Now that the town has elected him sheriff, he needs a woman who understands hard work and dedication. I have just the woman in mind."

THE END

DEAR READER

Want to read a free short story?
Sign up for our newsletter today!
https://www.ellie-rhodes.com/newsletter

Subscribers will be the first to learn when
the next book in the series will be released.

Did you enjoy *Better Together*?
Please visit the retailer's product page
if you enjoyed this story to leave a review.

Honest reviews of our books help
bring them to the attention of other readers.
We would be grateful if you could
spend a few minutes leaving a review.
Thank you!

Feel free to drop us a line.
Interacting with our readers is a highlight of our day,
I promise you'll get a reply, and I promise it will be from us.

ABOUT THE AUTHOR

Ellie Rhodes is an identical twin author duo who write *sweet with a little heat,* small-town romance novels. They love writing about strong, independent, fun, and flirty women and swoon-worthy men who make them laugh (they hope they make you laugh too!) They both have husbands who are their real-life heroes and who put up with, what their husbands refer to as, their "twin speak" (never endless mind-reading looks and bursts of uncontrollable laughter). When they aren't writing, both can completely lose track of time reading a good book and enjoy their summers outside after being holed-up over the long winter months.

www.ellie-rhodes.com
facebook.com/ellie.rhodes.718689
instagram.com/author_ellie_rhodes

ALSO BY ELLIE RHODES

DEER CREEK FALLS SERIES

Catch Me

Runaway Groom

Better Together

Made in the USA
Middletown, DE
24 January 2022

58394943R00120